"Do you have any idea how beautiful you are?" Drew...

"Be serious, Dre...

He leaned a sho... "I am. Very serious... think I've ever wanted a woman more. Not the way I want you."

Such dangerous words, she thought, so sincere. Dangerous because she wanted to believe them, and so sincere her pulse raced with the possibilities. But the treacherous emotions his touch aroused made her feel out of control. She had to deny them, or lose herself.

"But I don't want you," she finally said, but her reply was too weak, too late.

Drew had watched all the doubts rush through her and bring sadness to her eyes. Gently he suggested, "Maybe you don't know what you want."

"Yes, I do," she said. "I want my freedom. I've spent all my life taking care of other people. I don't want to do that anymore. You and Noah are not what I want."

"Then maybe we're what you *need*," he told her softly. She needed someone who would take care of her for a change, someone who wanted all that passion she kept bottled up inside. She needed someone to love her.

"You're wrong about that," she argued, more calmly than she felt.

"I don't think so." Drew resorted to fighting dirty—she left him no choice. As his gaze flicked over her body, reminding both of them how she responded to his touch, "I think I'm exactly what you need. . . ."

WHAT ARE *LOVESWEPT* ROMANCES?

They are stories of true romance and touching emotion. We believe those two very important ingredients are constants in our highly sensual and very believable stories in the LOVESWEPT *line. Our goal is to give you, the reader, stories of consistently high quality that may sometimes make you laugh, sometimes make you cry, but are always fresh and creative and contain many delightful surprises within their pages.*

Most romance fans read an enormous number of books. Those they truly love, they keep. Others may be traded with friends and soon forgotten. We hope that each LOVESWEPT *romance will be a treasure—a "keeper." We will always try to publish*

LOVE STORIES YOU'LL NEVER FORGET
BY AUTHORS YOU'LL ALWAYS REMEMBER

The Editors

Loveswept ®723

DOC
HOLIDAY

DEBRA
DIXON

BANTAM BOOKS
NEW YORK · TORONTO · LONDON · SYDNEY · AUCKLAND

DOC HOLIDAY

A Bantam Book / January 1995

*If you would be interested in receiving protective vinyl covers for your
Loveswept books, please write to this address for information:*

Loveswept
Bantam Books
P.O. Box 985
Hicksville, NY 11802

ISBN 0-553-44432-8

Published simultaneously in the United States and Canada

*Bantam Books are published by Bantam Books, a division of Bantam Dou-
bleday Dell Publishing Group, Inc. Its trademark, consisting of the words
"Bantam Books" and the portrayal of a rooster, is Registered in U.S.
Patent and Trademark Office and in other countries. Marca Registrada.
Bantam Books, 1540 Broadway, New York, New York 10036.*

PRINTED IN THE UNITED STATES OF AMERICA

OPM   0 9 8 7 6 5 4 3 2 1

For Beth de Guzman, who knows all
about little boys and Christmas

ONE

"Bah, humbug," Taylor Bishop whispered as she shut the door behind her. The December cold was easier to take than the Christmas chaos that reigned inside the house.

Every year she swore she'd get through the holidays without killing anyone, and every year she contemplated murder within twenty-four hours of crossing the threshold of her childhood home. While the urge to strangle her many siblings and widowed father had become something of a tradition, she didn't remember the compulsion ever being this strong.

Taylor leaned her forehead against the door's cold stained-glass oval and sighed. She loved her family. She did. Really. But right now she didn't like them very much.

Not a one of them had lifted a finger to organize Christmas. Not even the ones who lived close to home. The decorations were still in the attic; no one had given a thought to the festival parade. Dad hadn't even bought the first present! A bunch of men might think eight days was plenty of time to pull the holiday together, but she wasn't convinced. In fact, the situation might well be hopeless. Taylor wasn't sure she was up to another Christmas just like the last one.

You're not as young as you used to be, Taylor. You can't expect to have as much energy, she reminded herself, and then straightened up with a jerk as she realized she'd insulted herself. Taylor looked at her blurry reflection in the brass knocker beside the door and said out loud, "Twenty-nine years old is not exactly over the hill, either!"

"But you are climbing, Mouse," teased a warm, utterly masculine voice from behind her.

Taylor sucked in a breath, and the starch went right out of her legs. She steadied herself with a hand on the doorknob. No one called her Mouse anymore. No one had *ever* called her Mouse except Drew Haywood, and the voice couldn't possibly belong to him. He'd moved away from this northern Arkansas patch of nowhere a long time ago . . . and never looked back.

"Mouse?" the voice asked again, uncertain this time.

Slowly she turned around, irrationally thankful for a good hair day, last month's diet, and the chance to show the object of her first serious crush that she'd grown up. That she wasn't Clay's pesky kid sister anymore. Unfortunately, she hadn't planned on the man packing the same sensual wallop today as he had when Clay first introduced him to the family.

Before she could scrounge a sophisticated facade out

of her bag of feminine tricks, the bottom fell out of her stomach. Witty words deserted her. Honest to a fault, she silently acknowledged that the English language had always been a bit of a problem in Drew's presence. As a teenager she had spent a whole lot more time look-ing *at* him than talking *to* him.

Unexpectedly fond half-forgotten memories floated to the surface, and nostalgia stole over her as she raised her eyes to his and smiled. Drew's familiar grin was the nicest surprise she'd had since coming home yesterday.

"Hello, Taylor," he said in a voice that could still pull quicksilver through her veins.

In the blink of an eye, she replaced the schoolgirl adjectives of "good-looking" and "tall" with more accu-rate tags, like "sensual mouth," "devastating gaze," "sexy five o'clock shadow," and "shoulders wide enough to cradle a woman's head and soak up her tears." Not that she had any tears to spill right now, but one never knew when broad shoulders would come in handy.

Suddenly Taylor sobered and reminded herself that his shoulders had already been tested. He had offered her comfort and in the process stolen a piece of her heart that she'd never been able to get back.

"Stolen" wasn't the right word. She'd given him that little piece of her heart. Unfortunately, he hadn't wanted it. Shaking off the embarrassing memory, Tay-lor abandoned the past for reality. She wasn't sixteen anymore, and she didn't need comforting. She didn't need a man; she didn't need the complications.

"Hello, Hayseed," she said, using the old name

she'd given him in retaliation for Mouse. "Long time no see."

Drew Haywood chuckled and decided that little Taylor Bishop had grown up with a vengeance. Not that he had any business noticing she could hold her own in a room full of dreams. Nope, he didn't have any business noticing at all. But that didn't stop him. It never had.

Her eyes were the same rainy-day blue he remembered; her mouth still generous; but she wasn't the much-too-young and adoring Taylor who'd smiled shyly at him and crept right into his heart. Her coltish movements had settled themselves into supple gestures that suggested grace without being too formal. Her naturally blond hair skimmed her shoulders and shimmered with sophisticated highlights. He could only hope her offbeat sense of humor had survived the transformation and lurked behind the mature, sensitive expression she offered him.

As silence stretched between them, Taylor didn't rush to fill the void with chatter. Nor did Drew, which made him wonder why neither of them was particularly anxious to mix the moment with conversation. Because of the cold, she flipped up the collar on her quilted denim jacket and put her hands into the pockets. Drew mirrored her movements as he huddled deeper in his sheepskin coat, never taking his eyes off her. The grown-up version of Taylor fascinated him, and so did the tension.

Finally she said, "Well, I guess you're back for Christmas."

"No." Drew was certain he saw disappointment flicker across her face before he added, "I'm back for good."

"You're back? For good?" Surprised, Taylor tried to envision Drew as a pillar of the small Arkansas community. It wasn't much of a stretch. In her imagination, he made a very good pillar—strong, committed, vital. She wondered if he was living in the big white, ivy-covered monster his parents owned two streets over or if he'd bought something else. "Clay never said a word."

"He doesn't know. We haven't kept in touch the last few years."

"That would explain it," she said.

"Yeah," Drew agreed. "It would."

Taylor nodded and made an "um" sound. They were out of conversation again.

Anyone else would have wondered why two old friends were having such a hard time making small talk, but not Drew. He knew why. He and Taylor weren't old friends. Their relationship had been a lot more complicated. She'd had a crush on him. He'd had feelings for her, feelings he had no business having. The one time he let down his guard, he'd felt like a dirty old man taking advantage of her grief to rob the cradle.

Looking at the woman in front of him, he knew he'd never have to think of her as Clay's little sister again. The six-year age difference that had created the original problem was now a moot point. She was twenty-nine, definitely out of the cradle, and all grown up. Not that it mattered. Even if she wasn't in love or involved with someone else, his timing was still lousy.

In the beginning she'd been six years too young; now she was six years too late. He had Noah to think about. All he'd ever wanted was a family. Now that he had a second chance, he was going to make the most of it. Even if that meant he had to ignore ancient, but potent, chemistry.

Taylor shifted her weight, drawing one foot back and bouncing the toe of her shoe off the painted concrete porch. "I suppose you're anxious to meet Martha—" As she broke off, she rubbed her hands together in glee, and her eyes lit up with a wait-until-you-hear-this-one twinkle. "Oh, you probably don't know! Clay's married!"

"Married? Never-say-die, never-say-marry *Clay* actually got married?"

"Not in church, but he did get married. None of us have met her, and all he'll say is that she's perfect. That I'm going to love her." Then she added, "If they ever get here. They're not coming until tomorrow. Which means you'll have to come back. Sorry."

"Don't be. I didn't come here to see Clay."

Taylor's heart thumped a hard beat. "You didn't?"

"No." There wasn't the slightest hesitation in his answer, and the tiny word seemed to hang in the air between them like a promise waiting to be claimed.

Good Lord, she admonished herself. She was doing it again. Letting herself create something from nothing. Sure, it'd be nice to have Drew groveling and apologizing for breaking her heart and begging her to give him a chance. But that wasn't about to happen. She really didn't want it to happen. She doubted he even knew that, once upon a time, he'd broken her tender young heart.

Refusing to let old teenage fantasies take over her common sense, Taylor asked bluntly, "You're not selling something, are you? Like life insurance or cemetery plots?"

"Cemetery plots!" Stunned, Drew looked at her for a second before he caught the twinkle in her blue eyes. Then he laughed. "I'm not selling anything. Would you believe I came looking for you?"

"Right," she said with a touch of friendly sarcasm, and patted him on the shoulder as she walked briskly past him. "Dad's inside. He'll be glad to see you. Just go on in. I was going for a walk before dark."

He watched her skip lightly down the steps and strike out across the yard, skirting the line of cars double parked in the wide drive. When she didn't so much as look back, he decided that the tension between them must have been his imagination. While he tried to figure out why that bothered him so much, she turned left and headed in the general direction of Main Street. That's when Drew remembered that he hadn't asked for the favor yet.

"Wait! I'll go with you." He easily vaulted the porch steps. The sharp contact with the frozen ground jarred him as he landed, but he didn't slow down. Taylor hadn't. Wishing for a muffler and gloves, he closed the distance between them to fall in beside her.

When he accidentally brushed her hand with his, she didn't snatch her hand back, but she did slip it in her pocket, away from temptation or out of harm's way.

He wasn't sure which. Without a doubt, Drew recognized the invisible line just drawn between them. He wondered if she was avoiding the past or if she was sidestepping the future. Either way, the No Trespassing sign had just been posted.

Fair enough. This Christmas was for Noah. And for himself, too, if he was perfectly honest. He wanted Noah to have a Christmas to hold on to, a Christmas to hug tight and remember when life wasn't perfect.

And he wanted Taylor to help him create that picture-book Christmas. She was a pro. No one "did" Christmas better than the Bishops. When her mother fell ill and then died, sixteen-year-old Taylor had kept the home fires burning and the heart of Christmas alive. That's what he wanted for Noah. He wanted the heart and soul he'd seen in the Bishop house. He wanted the magic Taylor knew how to create. He wanted her to teach him how to be a family.

Drew supposed he could just blurt out his request, but instinct warned him that he'd have a better chance with Taylor if he eased into the subject. With that in mind, he said, "It's getting colder."

Taylor slanted a glance at him and wondered what the heck had gone wrong with her graceful exit. The man was supposed to have taken the hint and disappeared inside the house. Instead he was shoulder to shoulder with her, walking along a narrow sidewalk cracked from haphazard maintenance and too many icy winters. Worse, he was so bored he had resorted to the weather as a topic of conversation.

"The radio said we'd have snow by midnight," she

added, and looked away to roll her eyes at the pitiful rejoinder.

"Snow," Drew repeated as though it were the most interesting subject imaginable. "Let me get this straight. It's not my imagination. It really is cold enough to snow."

"Yes."

"Good Lord, Mouse, all you've got on is that short jacket! Why are you out here walking instead of inside next to that big fireplace in the family room and drinking homemade eggnog?"

Taylor noticed not only that he called her Mouse, but that his tone questioned her common sense. Her feminine pride decided she'd have to do something about that if he kept it up. She had six brothers who were more than capable of scolding her. She didn't need another one. As evenly as she could, she told him, "The jacket was handy, and I have very good reasons for being out here in this cold."

"And they are?"

Taylor had to laugh at the stern question. She stopped and put her hands on her hips before she said, "None of your business."

Drew grimaced. "I used the I'm-the-grown-up-and-I-know-best voice, didn't I?"

"Yeah. You did."

Taking her elbow, Drew pulled her forward. "What if I promised never to do that again?"

Taylor smiled and let herself be pulled along by his firm, steady tug. "Then maybe I'd tell you."

"Then tell me. Because I want to know why being

out here is more fun than being inside a house that smells like Christmas. I'm dying of curiosity. Really."

"Liar," she accused softly. He knew full well the chaos inside the Bishop household. He'd been a part of it for a number of years. For a couple of those years, the family had even joked that they were going to have to hang a stocking for him, since he was around so much.

After she gently disengaged his hand from the crook of her arm, Taylor dug some thin red mittens out of her jacket pockets. As she pushed her hands inside them, she told him, "I'm out here for lots of reasons."

"Like what kind of reasons?"

"Like Mother Nature played a cruel, nasty trick on me and slowed down my metabolism last year. I either have to walk or give up eating. Walking seemed the best choice," she said with a resigned sigh.

"Good decision." Drew swept his gaze down the length of her body, admiring the snug fit of her blue jeans, which were not quite new but not yet faded. Her curves were in all the right places, but it was her style that made her sexy, the easy way she moved and laughed. She was soft and warm and didn't have the slightest idea of how the chilly air had rouged her cheeks and reddened her mouth.

Pretending not to notice the impact she made on his senses had been difficult enough when she was sixteen. It was going to be damn near impossible now. Especially when he thought even the absurd Rudolph pin on her jacket was sexy. A tiny chain dangled from the pin, inviting him to pull it and light up the reindeer's red nose. Instead of using the chain as an excuse to touch her, he kept his hands to himself and said, "Okay, exercise is one reason. You said there were lots. What else?"

"Dad told me there'd been some changes in the neighborhood and in the Square since last time I was here. I wanted to see for myself." Taylor paused and looked around the old neighborhood of custom-built homes and tall trees. "I didn't realize he meant there were fences."

Beside them an attractive brick-post and rail fence bordered the Andersons' yard. Ahead of them a wrought iron fence followed the edge of another yard and marched smartly around the corner. "These weren't here last year. When we went caroling, we gathered around the Andersons' front door." She let one unpolished nail trail along a brick. "I guess we'll be singing from the street this year. It won't feel right."

Noting the wistful tone in her voice, Drew said, "You always did have definite ideas about how things were supposed to be."

She shrugged. "I might live in Little Rock, but this is still home. Part of me wants everything to always be the way I remember it."

"Do you want people to be the way you remember them?"

"Some of them."

"Am I the way you remembered?"

"No." Her answer was quick and sharp. Too quick, too sharp.

"And are you disappointed?"

"Not exactly." That was true. Sort of. She was disappointed that he could still rattle her, but not that he was better than her memories. Taylor tucked her hands behind her back and smiled at the ground. Let him figure that out. She wasn't going to explain it.

"How long is this little stroll going to be?" Drew asked as they reached the corner.

"Tired already?" she asked innocently and stopped. "Oh . . . I forgot. You *are* older than me."

"Not that much," he ground out. "I'm not senile yet. So why don't you tell me the real reason we're taking this walk? You don't look like you need the exercise, and you could have toured the town from a car. What gives?"

Taylor rubbed her mitten-covered palms together. She recalled the long ago birthday her family had forgotten. The only person who'd asked her what was wrong or noticed she was upset had been Drew. "Never could fool you, huh?"

"Never could fool me," Drew echoed softly, the cold frosting his words as he spoke. He leaned closer and reached out to grasp Rudolph's chain. The back of his hand rubbed lightly against her breast as he pulled downward.

When the reindeer's nose lit up, so did Taylor's internal warning lights. Whatever was happening right now had nothing to do with the past. The man in front of her was causing all of the tingling and pulse pounding.

Compared to the flesh-and-blood man, the memories were vague. Drew was too real, too much, too soon. He was trouble. He was the kind of man she could fall in love with, and love was not in Taylor's plan. Love was dangerous. Love led to commitment and family. She didn't want that. Raising one family had been enough.

"Why are we out here, Taylor?" he asked.

When she didn't answer, he tilted up her chin, forcing her eyes to meet his. She never could fool Drew. What was the use in trying? He'd just keep at her until she confessed the truth.

She pulled her head away and started toward the city park across the street. "Because I thought a walk was preferable to a life sentence for murdering my family."

Drew's honest laughter made her smile, and so did his question. "What would your motive have been?"

"Self-defense. My brothers are driving me crazy."

Drew thought about that, studied her profile. "You look fairly sane to me."

"Not for long."

"Want to tell me about it?"

"Want to listen?" she asked skeptically.

"Cross my heart." Drew suited action to words and made the sign on his chest.

"It isn't a pretty picture." Taylor furrowed her brow as though thinking hard. "Let's see . . . where should I start?" Her youngest brother came to mind immediately. "Oh, I know! Mikey's quitting college. I think he's doing it because they want to throw him out and he doesn't want to give them the satisfaction."

Drew ducked under a branch that hung over the sidewalk like an arbor. "Why should that drive you crazy? He wouldn't be the first kid who opted out of college for real life."

"He will in this family. Momma wanted all of us to

get an education. I promised her that we would, and I refuse to let Mikey be my only failure."

The park spread out before them, winter brown and dusted with the leftover leaves of fall. Skeleton trees stood guard over deserted swing sets and slides. Drew inclined his head toward the empty gazebo that held a place of honor on the far side of the park.

When Taylor agreed with his choice, he said, "Okay, Mikey's a problem. What else?"

"Don't you mean *who* else?" Taylor corrected.

"Ah . . . my mistake. Who else?"

"Bo. He and Becky are expecting baby number four. Neither of them have considered the fact that child care will be more than Becky earns at the bank here in town. And then there's David, who appears to have just realized the distinction between antique and old. He's wandering around Dad's house putting names on the furniture so we won't be fighting over who gets what when Dad dies."

Taylor flicked the back of her hand across Drew's biceps when he began to chuckle. "None of this is funny, Hayseed."

"Oh, yes it is. I was worried about you, Mouse. I thought maybe you'd changed, but I can see that you haven't. Beneath that very pretty exterior still beats the heart of a pragmatist. Family first and to hell with everything else."

"Well, someone's got to do it!"

"And that somebody has to be you."

"Not if you've got some other fool willing to take this family off my hands!" she shot back.

"Caring about your family doesn't make you a fool," he told her as they reached the large octagonal structure. "It's one of the things that makes you Taylor."

"Right," she said, and grabbed a post as she perched on the sturdy latticework railing that rimmed the base of the gazebo. "Being the family slave is such an attractive quality. I'll be sure to put it in the personal section of my résumé the next time I'm looking for a job."

He propped a hip against the railing and lost the thread of the conversation. The railing was cold, and all he could think about was the contrast of Taylor's warm bottom and the cold wood.

Almost as if she could read his thoughts, she hopped down and brushed absently at her rump. The red mittens didn't take the edge off Drew's enjoyment. He was really going to have to get a grip on his imagination if Taylor agreed to help him. He couldn't spend the next eight days lusting after the Christmas consultant.

Or could he?

"Enough about me." She took a few steps, whirled, and paced back toward him. "Why are *you* back in town? I never thought you'd come back."

"I came back because Harvey, Arkansas, is the last place on earth that my ex-wife is likely to visit."

"You have a wife?" Her question was soft and shocked. He didn't "feel" married.

"Not anymore."

"I knew that," Taylor said quickly. It was just that she'd never thought of him with a wife, never asked Clay about his old friend, never wanted to know. She tugged her jacket. "I was just surprised. You and Clay said you'd never get married."

"People change. Priorities change."

Taylor knew he was talking about more than a youthful vow. He was talking about his marriage. "How long have you been divorced?"

"A long time."

"Bad divorce?" she asked, knowing it was too personal a question and unable to stop herself from asking.

Drew nodded, thinking about five-year-old Noah. His son had been less than a year old when Anna had taken him halfway around the world. He'd seen Noah as often as he could, but the distance had made it impossible to be a real part of Noah's life, impossible to be the kind of father he wanted to be. Now that he finally had him back, this would be their first real holiday—first week before Christmas, first Christmas Eve, first trip to Santa Claus, first Christmas morning. "You could say it was a bad divorce. She took everything I cared about."

"I'm sorry."

"I wasn't. I was mad as hell."

Winter wasn't any colder than the anger she saw flicker in Drew's eyes. So many years, and still so much feeling, Taylor thought. She whispered, "You must have loved her a lot."

Drew smiled without humor and told the truth. "Not enough. Not the way I was supposed to. I married the wrong woman." Casting a speculative look at Taylor, he asked, "Now that I've bared my soul, what about you? Are you divorced, single, or just don't wear a ring?"

Holding up a red mitten, Taylor reported, "No ring, no husband, no chains."

"Chains?"

"You know, family ties . . . the ones that bind and gag?" she joked and tried to tuck her hair behind her ear before she realized that feat was nearly impossible to accomplish while wearing mittens.

"That's not going to work, Mouse." Drew closed the distance between them and pushed her hand away.

His fingertips were cold against her skin as he traced the shell of her ear, tucking hair smoothly in place. A shiver raced up her spine as his knuckles rested along the side of her neck and his thumb traced the line of her jaw. Along with the shiver came the realization that she'd never married because she'd never been tempted. Not trusting her eyes to keep her body's secrets, Taylor focused on the deep purple shirt she could see in the vee of Drew's coat.

"Still so soft," he said when she didn't move away.

Hesitantly she said, "Excuse m-me?"

"Your skin was always so soft. So were you, Taylor. And warm." His thumb wandered to the corner of her mouth. "That's what I remember most when I think about you."

She cleared her throat and backed away to put a little distance between her teenage fantasies and reality. *Don't believe everything you hear,* Taylor told herself. He was teasing her. *Then why does he look so damn serious?* Because he was always good at teasing.

As brightly as she could, she grinned at him. "Nice try, but we both know you didn't give me a thought until you came to see Clay and stumbled on me. Heck, you probably called me Mouse because you couldn't remember my—

"Taylor Marie Bishop."

"—name," she ended lamely. "Lucky guess."

"Two brothers are older. Four are younger. Your birthday is October 7. Unless your tastes have changed, you like Cream of Wheat, not oatmeal." He paused and then asked, "Do I need to go on? I came looking for you, Taylor."

"Why?" A weak question but the only one she could get out.

"Your name is at the top of my favorite people list."

Tilting her head as though doubting his sincerity, she shamelessly fished for a compliment. "Me? You expect me to believe I was at the top of your list? Why not Cissy Caldwell or Leigh Madison? If my memory serves, you were wild about the two of them."

"If memory serves, I was wild about you." Drew meant to match her light teasing tone, but something happened between his brain and his mouth. The words came out a touch too husky, a touch too serious. Years ago he'd been wild about the idea of what Taylor would *become*. Today he was confronted with reality, and it surpassed his expectation. Leaning closer, bringing his gaze level with hers, he said, "Face it, Taylor. I came looking for you."

TWO

Disbelief and satisfaction unfurled in the pit of Taylor's stomach. Lord, it was so silly to like this feeling of power that was welling up inside of her. But she did. She liked it a lot. All because Drew Haywood had come looking for her.

Taylor had to admit that the prospect of being pursued by Drew tempted her with interesting possibilities for a little good-natured revenge. She hadn't exactly been nursing a broken heart all these years, but neither had she gotten over her silly childhood attachment to him. That much had been painfully obvious when she turned around and found him on her porch.

Maybe this Christmas was the perfect time to get him out of her system.

"You found me." Her voice was intentionally provocative, heavily Southern, as she added, "Now what *are* you going to do with me?"

Her question slammed into Drew's gut. About a

dozen libido-driven impulses rampaged through his mind. He gritted his teeth against the temptation to act on any of them. *You have made a mistake, buddy. A big mistake. What made you think you could mix Noah's Christmas with your feelings for Taylor without sacrificing one for the other?*

His goals as Noah's parent warred with his goals as a man. The man wanted to respond to the teasing challenge in Taylor's eyes by kissing her; the parent knew better than to complicate the situation. Noah deserved to have his dad's complete attention.

And so does Taylor, a sneaky voice inside his head whispered. Ignoring the voice wasn't easy, but he had too much at stake in his life to take a detour down memory lane. If he did, he might never get back on track. Noah was still reeling from a mother who had abandoned him rather than alienate her new spouse. Drew didn't want to be the kind of father who conveniently forgot his son every time the sex drive kicked in.

Drew blinked once slowly and cursed his lousy timing. He took a step back. Being a single parent was going to be harder than he thought, in more ways than one. "I need a favor, Taylor."

"I give you a great line like that and all you can come up with is 'I need a favor'!" She stabbed a mitten in his direction and made "tut-tut" noises. "You are slipping, Hayseed."

"Being a father will do that to you."

The news that Drew had a child effectively burst Taylor's bubble. All the pleasure of flirting with Drew was sucked back down into the pit of her stomach, lying there like a lead weight. Just when Christmas was beginning to look up, the black cloud hovering over her began to rain trouble.

Drew was definitely trouble. She didn't get involved with men who had children . . . although part of her seemed willing to make an exception in Drew's case. *No!* Taylor put her mental foot down. Ready-made families weren't her style. Neither were brand-new, do-it-yourself families. She'd already raised one family, she reminded herself.

"Boy or girl?" she asked, and wandered aimlessly around the inside of the gazebo, pretending to check out the rest of the park.

"A boy. Noah. He's five."

When she heard the name, Taylor paused for a half second in mid-stride. Noah. A great name. It was high on the list of names she had picked out for the kids she never expected to have.

She loved children; she just never planned on having any of her own. When a baby attack hit, she visited her nieces and nephews until the yearning was gone. Given the unruly temperaments of her two nieces and three nephews, baby attacks didn't last very long. However, they were happening more often as she got closer to the big three-oh.

"Noah's not a name you hear very much anymore," she said as she finished the slow circling of the perimeter.

"No, it's not." Drew blew on his hands and rubbed them together. "But he was born in the middle of a five-day torrential downpour. Noah seemed appropriate."

Taylor laughed in spite of herself. "Very appropriate."

"Anna would disagree with you."

"Then the woman has absolutely no sense of humor," she declared, and stopped beside him. "Who's Anna?"

"My ex-wife."

"Oh. I should have guessed. Sorry."

"Why should you be sorry? It's true. Anna didn't have a funny bone in her body. That's one of the reasons I'm thankful that Noah lives with me now."

Oh, Lord, he wants a favor, she remembered. *If he asks me to baby-sit, I'll deck him. I swear I will.* It was bad enough being at the beck and call of her father and brothers because they didn't believe she had anything better to do than organize their holiday, but to have Drew Haywood ask her to baby-sit would be mortifying.

"I bet he's a great kid," she managed to say with some enthusiasm.

"I think so. He's a little on the quiet side, but I think he'll come around."

Taylor stared. "Why on earth would you want him to? Once they start making noise, they never stop. Never. Put tape over his mouth before it's too late."

"I don't recall any tape over Jason's and Mikey's mouths," he said drily.

"By the time I figured out why Momma kept duct tape in the kitchen drawer, it was too late!"

"So you wouldn't be concerned about his being quiet?" he asked intently.

She crossed her arms and raised an eyebrow. The man was serious; he was actually worried, and his eyes were shadowed. So she quit teasing him and asked, "Does Noah talk?"

"Yes."

"In complete sentences?"

"Yes."

"Does he make sense?"

"Yes."

"Then give him a couple of years. You'll be begging for duct tape. If you're really worried, I can get him one of those fireman helmets with a real siren on top. Once he flips that switch, the kid will make enough noise to drive you batty in no time. Guaranteed."

The tension around Drew's mouth relaxed a little, and he said, "I think I'll pass on the helmet."

"Smart man."

"I came looking for you, didn't I?" That husky, intimate quality was back in his voice, and he seemed quite pleased with himself, as if he'd just discovered a secret.

She didn't even realize she was backing away from him until her rump made contact with the gazebo edge. She'd run out of room, and he was closing the distance between them, pursuing her. "You came looking for me because you want a favor."

"Among other things." He braced his hand against one of the posts as if it were the most natural thing in the world for him to stand so close to her. The glimmer in his eyes matched the huskiness of his voice. Around them, winter was creeping into the park, dropping the temperature, but Taylor could have sworn that the temperature in the gazebo was rising.

She inhaled deeply, sucking frigid air into her lungs, amazed at how cold it was outside her body and yet how hot inside. She tried not to pay any attention to her hormones, which liked having a big, strong man look at her as if she were the only woman on the planet. Despite her determination, her question came out slightly breathless. "What's the . . . favor you need?"

"I need a Taylor Bishop Christmas."

His answer was so unexpected, she felt like she'd stepped off a bus while it was still moving. She wondered if she'd heard him correctly. "You need a what? I'm afraid you lost me."

Drew hoped not. With every passing second, he was more certain that Taylor was the kind of woman that a man would be a fool to lose. She cared about family, and that was something he wanted—a real family, a family that fought, and cried, and loved each other anyway. He wanted to turn his house into a home. Deep down inside where it counted, Taylor knew what made a family. And how to drive him crazy.

Right now she was flustered and sexy. He couldn't seem to drag his attention away from her mouth, which was slightly parted. The small, ragged breaths she took created enticing puffs of frost when warm air met cold. This was how he remembered her, gorgeous on the outside and warm on the inside. He remembered kissing her once. He wanted to kiss her again.

Before he could, she bolted underneath his arm, exclaiming, "Oh, look! It's snowing." She almost raced out of the gazebo and away from him. "I love the snow."

"I know," Drew said heavily. "I remember that too."

By the time he joined her, she was holding out her hands to catch snowflakes on the red wool of her mittens. Her innocent gesture reminded him of Noah and why he'd really come looking for her. "Come on. I'll walk you home and explain about the favor."

"Good, because I want to know exactly what a Taylor Bishop Christmas is. Unless it's one fraught with complications, I haven't a clue." Taylor dusted snowflakes off her mittens and looked at him.

Drew shrugged and started walking. "That's the problem. If I knew what it was, I wouldn't need the favor. All I know is that I want Noah to have the same kind of Christmas that you and your brothers had."

"What on earth for? The tree was always—"

"Lopsided and tied to the wall," Drew finished for her.

"My point exactly!"

"But they smelled great. I coveted those trees." He paused at the edge of the street, waiting for a truck to pass. "On the other hand, our tree was perfect—artificial, silver, and symmetrically decorated with pink and blue satin balls. If Mother was feeling particularly festive, she added a gold garland."

When an expression of distaste settled on Taylor's face, he said, "And that's *my* point exactly."

"What point—oh! I understand now. You want me to break the news to your mother," she surmised as they crossed the street. "No way, Hayseed. You don't like your mother's tree, you tell her yourself."

"I don't need to tell her. Dad retired the minute I said I'd move home and take over the bank. They moved to Florida a month ago. It's just me and Noah in the house now."

"They're not coming home for Christmas?"

"Nope."

Bewildered, Taylor told him, "Then you can have any kind of tree you want! You don't need me. Go down to the Boy Scout tree lot and take your chance like the rest of us."

"And what comes after I buy the tree?"

"Decorations."

"I know that. But what kind and how many?"

Taylor stared at him. "Whatever kind you like and as many as you like."

"I want the kind you have. I like those. Where do I get them?"

An uneasy feeling began to make the hairs on the back of Taylor's neck stand up. The ornaments on the Bishop tree were a collection of handmade keepsakes, ancient store-bought trimmings, and homemade gingerbread men, baked fresh each Christmas. A tree like theirs couldn't be bought; it had to evolve over the years.

"Drew, don't you have some ornaments? Haven't you ever put up a Christmas tree?"

"No."

"Never? But you were married! You have a son!"

"I've never had him for Christmas."

"You never had him for Christmas?" she echoed. "But—"

"We were divorced before Noah was a year old. Because of his age, Anna got full custody, and then she moved to Europe."

Bad divorce?

You could say it was a bad divorce. She took everything I cared about.

"Anna showed up in Arizona about two months ago, right after she got married again. She had Noah and a suitcase with her." His voice hardened, took on an edge that was dangerous. "It seems that Noah was cramping her new husband's style. She made it very clear where her priorities were. She didn't need the child support anymore, so she didn't need Noah. In less than a day, I had custody papers drawn up and my ex-wife back on a plane. Noah's mine now."

Taylor cut off the wave of empathy that rolled over her. She had enough to do this Christmas without worrying about Drew and Noah. As touching as Drew's plight was, she couldn't—she wouldn't—get into a situation like this. The caring tone of his voice made it clear that any woman in his life would have to accept the fact that he and Noah were a package deal.

No matter how many emotions, old and new, that he stirred in her, she wasn't in the market for a package deal. She'd put her life on hold once before when a man with small children needed her. From the time she was fourteen, she'd been both mother and sister to her younger brothers. She hadn't started college until she was twenty-four, and even then she felt like she had to come home every weekend, every holiday.

Mikey, the youngest, had been five years old when their mother got sick and only seven when she died. How was she supposed to tell a scared seven-year-old that tucking him into bed conflicted with a hot date? How was she supposed to tell the boys that she didn't have time to bake the cookies Santa Claus expected every year? How was she supposed to ignore the promises she made to her mother? She couldn't. The boys needed her.

Taylor admired Drew's commitment, but it wasn't one she was willing to make again. As selfish as the notion was, she wanted some time for herself, to find her own happiness and establish herself in her career. Now that Mikey was in college, it was finally time to let go of the family responsibilities, not take them on all over again!

"If you don't have any ornaments from the past," she told him bluntly, "I guess you'll have to start from scratch. It's not as difficult as it looks. Just buy a tree and slap some ornaments on it."

"That's what my mother did. That's what Anna did. It was pretty, but it wasn't Christmas."

To hold back her heartfelt agreement, Taylor pressed her lips together. This wasn't her fight. She didn't have the time.

Drew put a hand on her arm and turned her to face him. His dark brown eyes bored into hers, and his brow was furrowed as if he were trying not to speak until he'd sorted out exactly what he wanted to say. He didn't even try to camouflage the emotion he felt.

"When I think of Christmas, I think of you. Whether you know it or not, you're special. I think of the way your house always smelled like spice and cinnamon. I remember coming in and looking at the tree and feeling connected somehow to the past and to the future. I remember leaving my house which was cold and formal and walking into your house which was full of warmth and laughter. I remember that cornbread dressing and coconut cake. I remember thinking, 'This is how I want my house to feel. This is how I want Christmas to taste.' Hell, that's how I wanted my *life* to feel!"

Her resolve was weakening and so were her knees. He was so close, so intense, so sure that she was special. "If you know what you want, then what's stopping you?"

"Because I remember the feeling, not the specifics. I need your help to re-create that feeling for Noah. I need you to show me what to do, how to do it, and when to do it. You always made it look so easy. You were so organized, everything just came together."

If he'd flung a handful of snow in her face, the cold wouldn't have stung her any more than his last sentence. *You were so organized, everything just came together.* Carefully Taylor pulled her arms out of his grasp and held on to her temper. She was special because she was *organized*?

Wasn't that exactly like a man! The men in her family anyway. Don't worry about Christmas; Taylor'll take care of it. Oh, yes! That was the Bishop family motto!

Apparently Drew was hoping to live by that credo too. He hadn't come looking for her out of friendship, lust, or even out of curiosity.

The truth was so humiliating. He'd come looking for her because she was useful, not because she was a truly special woman or because he felt anything for her. With every step she took toward home, she reminded herself of that fact.

Thirty minutes ago, she'd been ready to sell her family to the first gypsy she saw. Now she was glad to have them as an excuse. She couldn't organize Drew's perfect Christmas, because she already had a family depending on her. She already had someone who expected her to be useful.

"I'm flattered."

"But." Drew let out a resigned breath, full of disappointment. "I hear a 'but.'"

"I'm afraid so. I wish I could help out," she lied smoothly. "Really I do, but I've got our Christmas to pull together. It's a madhouse this year, what with Clay bringing his new wife, the house to decorate at the last minute, presents to buy, grocery shopping . . ." She let her voice trail off.

"And that doesn't leave you much time to spend with your family."

Taylor blinked. Time? She never had quiet time to spend with her family, but she jumped on the excuse anyway. "Right. Not to mention that Dad hasn't even started on the float for the Christmas Parade. Well, technically it's the high school float, but since he's the coach, you know it's always been a family project."

"I see." His tone implied that he didn't see at all. "Of course, a high school float's more important than one small boy whose mother abandoned him."

"Look, I'm sorry, Drew, but—" she began quickly.

"No, no. Don't be. I should have known—your family comes first. I can't fault you for that. This Christmas I wanted Noah to be happy, so I gave it a shot. It didn't work out, but you can't blame a guy for trying."

The smile he gave her was genuine and understanding. It also made her feel about two inches tall. Why did Drew have to be so damn classy? Why did he have to be a father? Guilt pinched her sharply until she saw the corner of his mouth twitch.

"Drew Haywood! You are deliberately trying to make me feel bad!"

"I know. Is it working?"

"Yes! No! How could you do that to me?"

"I have a son who's depending on me."

Taylor groaned in frustration and kicked the brittle leaves that had drifted into piles along the sidewalk and were now covered with a light dusting of snow. "Drew, I can't. I would if I could. But I can't."

That much was true even if her reasons weren't quite what he thought they were. "Look, if you need advice about something or have a question, you can call me. And why don't you bring Noah over for a visit sometime? To see the house and the tree? In fact, come for Christmas dinner. It'll be like old times."

"Not quite."

There was a predatory gleam in his eyes that caused

her to swallow before she reminded herself that Drew's interest in her was purely platonic. He needed her, but he didn't *want* her. However, he wasn't a bit above charming her to get what he wanted. She'd be foolish to forget that. "Maybe not quite like old times. We've all changed over the years."

"Grown up, Taylor. Grown up."

"That too."

Drew walked her to the porch and stopped her before she went up the steps. "Thanks for the invitation, Mouse. I really appreciate it. This is important to me." He seemed about to say something and then changed his mind. "Listen, I've got to get back to Noah. I told the sitter I'd only be gone an hour. You tell Clay congratulations and to call me when he has some time. We'll get together."

"I will." Unexpectedly Taylor found herself right back where she started—on her front porch, facing the prospect of another Christmas and wondering where all the magic had gone. A tiny voice inside her head told her that if she was looking for magic, she shouldn't have said no to Drew.

"Bah, humbug," she whispered, and watched Drew until he'd turned the corner, heading toward his house and Noah. When she pushed open her own front door, she promised herself she wouldn't kill anyone tonight. At least not until they'd brought all the decorations down from the attic.

Even in the entrance hall she could hear the sounds of a polite disagreement coming from the dining room. Judging from the comments, the difference of opinion centered around an incorrect answer to a nature and science question from Trivial Pursuit. She tuned out the argument with no trouble, but as she turned to hang her jacket up, she saw a little sticker with initials on the walnut coat tree.

That did it! She might not kill anyone, but she was definitely going to have a little chat with David about his morbid fascination with divvying up the family antiques.

The scent of bacon penetrated her consciousness first. Then the aroma of coffee filtered through. Taylor sat straight up in the canopied twin bed she'd slept in for most of her life. Bacon? Coffee? Something was wrong. The only person who ever fixed Sunday breakfast at the Bishop house was Taylor Bishop. Good Lord! If Jason was trying to cook again, they'd have a four-alarm fire before too long.

She tossed off the covers, sucking in her breath as the cold air hit her bare legs. Too late she remembered her dad hardly ever turned the heater above sixty-two at night. She put on a pair of red socks and grabbed the green flannel robe from the foot of her bed before she opened her door and surveyed the upstairs hallway. All the bedroom doors were closed, which usually meant everyone was still asleep. So who was doing the cooking?

Puzzled, Taylor hurried downstairs, belting her robe as she went. Boxes of decorations still sat in the middle of the living room floor waiting for a tree, but the oak table in the dining room had been cleared of last night's trivia game and set with place mats and silverware. When an off-key *feminine* humming emanated from the kitchen, Taylor decided she was in the Twilight Zone. That was the only possible explanation for bacon, coffee, place mats, and humming.

Warily Taylor stuck her head in the doorway. A tall, auburn-haired woman was cracking eggs with one hand and reaching for a cup of coffee with the other. The sight of an unfamiliar woman making herself at home was startling enough, but the redhead's first words were more so.

"I thought you'd be the first one up. Well, stop gaping at me, Taylor, and come on in. I'm Martha. Your new sister-in-law. I'm normally a hugger, but my hands are full. I've had the devil of a time finding everything."

Instead of delight, Taylor was shocked to realize she felt her territory had somehow been invaded. The clutter she hadn't been able to face last night was now nonexistent. The pale blue countertops which ordinarily looked dull and scuffed now shone with a new life. Dishes were neatly stacked and drying in the wire rack beside the sink. What looked like homemade biscuits were neatly lined up on a cookie sheet, waiting for the oven.

Stifling perverse resentment, Taylor walked all the way into the kitchen and combed her fingers through her hair. "How'd you know it was me? Clay didn't say anything about you having eyes in the back of your head."

"I don't." Martha tossed an eggshell into the disposal, confirming that she was an obsessively neat cook. "Men are never that quiet. And when it comes to noise, the Bishop men are in a class all by themselves. If Clay and I have any boys, I'm taping their mouths shut."

A chuckle finally escaped Taylor, and the territorial feeling eased up a bit. "Oh, I think I'm going to like you."

"Good, because Clay promised me I'd like you." Martha cracked another egg as she looked over her shoulder. She had blue eyes and the kind of bone structure that most women would kill for. No wonder her brother had fallen so fast and so hard—Martha was gorgeous.

"And Clay promised me that you were perfect." Taylor grinned.

"He obviously exaggerates. As you can see, I have crow's feet around my eyes, and I'm carrying around fifteen pounds that belong to someone else. Hey, can you slip my biscuits in the oven?"

"Oh . . . of course." Taylor moved toward the stove, wondering how she could feel like a fifth wheel in her own kitchen. "When did the two of you get in?"

"Really late last night." Martha rummaged in the refrigerator for some butter for cooking the eggs. "I didn't see any reason to wait until today to make the trip. When we got here, you were already asleep. I refused to let them wake you, since you're going to need all the rest you can get."

"That's true enough"—Taylor picked up a fork and began turning the bacon—"but do you mind telling me how *you* knew that?"

"Lord! That was easy. I took one look at this house and said to myself, 'It's a wonder that girl hasn't killed them all.' Dear sweet Clay didn't understand why I was upset. He actually told me not to worry about Christmas. That you'd take care of everything."

Martha rolled her eyes and sliced some butter into the skillet to melt. "Can you believe it? As if I'd let you do all this by yourself now that I'm here!"

Although her sister-in-law was on her side, Taylor wasn't sure whether to be pleased or irritated. That little territorial streak was back again. It was one thing to admit to herself that the magic had gone out of Christmas, and entirely another to hand over the responsibility to someone else. As long as she could remember, Christmas was the holiday that meant the most to her brothers. Christmas was the one thing that hadn't changed when her mother died. She hadn't let it.

"Thanks, Martha, but you're a guest. You shouldn't—"

"Honey, I'm family now. I realize that Bo and Tim and their wives have their own places to decorate and the kids to look out for, but this is 'Christmas Central' for me and Clay. I'm going to help and that's all there is to it." Martha winked at her as if everything were settled. "Clay'll be down in a minute and then we can sit down to a nice breakfast. Just the three of us. Before the rest of 'em get up."

Taylor flicked her eyes toward the bowl of eggs that her sister-in-law was expertly whipping into a creamy yellow mixture. "Since when does Clay eat scrambled eggs?"

"Since I burnt the first ones I tried to fry." Martha gave her a mischievous look. "I just couldn't get that flip thing right. I'm much better at scrambling. It's so much easier."

Taylor stopped poking at the shriveling bacon and put her knuckles against her hips. "I don't believe this! You burn a couple of eggs and Clay changes a thirty-five-year-old eating habit? I tried for years but he wouldn't touch an egg unless it was fried."

"You're not married to him. You can't lock him out of the bedroom." Martha smiled as she poured egg mixture into the heated skillet. "On the other hand, I can."

She's right, Taylor thought. Whether she meant to send a message or not, her sister-in-law couldn't have been more plain—a wife was more important to a man than a sister. Mother and wife would always come first on a man's list of the important women in his life. The order might vary but those were always numbers one and two. Sister ranked a distant third.

Taylor waved to her dad and brothers and pushed Martha out the door. "Believe me, I'll be fine. You go to church with the rest of them. Clay wants to show you off."

Before her new sister could argue anymore, Taylor smiled sweetly and closed the door in her face. Sighing, she realized she had the house to herself for a couple of hours. After that, Martha, who was showing signs of pit bull tenacity, would be back and ready to help. Somehow the thought was depressing rather than cheering.

Stop whining, she told herself. First a shower, then she'd sort through the decorations. A half hour later she was kneeling beside the first box when the doorbell rang.

"What is this? A conspiracy?" she mumbled as she went to answer it. "I'm never going to get anything done."

Drew stood on the porch looking slightly rumpled, just like a dad who'd been playing in the snow with his son. A thick spiral notebook hung loosely from one hand. Involuntarily she looked behind him for Noah.

"He's not with me."

"Clay's not here," she said quickly.

"Why do you always assume I'm here to see Clay?"

"Aren't you?"

"No."

"Then why are you here?"

"Other than the fact you kept me up all night?"

"Me?"

"Yes."

"Why?"

That was a question Drew had been asking himself. Well, he knew the answer; he just didn't like it. The thoughts that kept him awake all night weren't noble dreams of home and family. They were fantasies of Taylor beneath him.

Ironically, what she was wearing right now didn't help any. She had a piece of tinsel in her hair. The white jogging pants were soft and baggy; the sweatshirt, embroidered with red *ho-ho-ho*'s, was too big. His overactive imagination was all too happy to fill in the details.

Controlling his imagination had been a problem since seeing her yesterday.

"Can I come in?"

She hesitated a second too long. "Sure."

In that extra second Drew knew they were headed for trouble. Whether or not they wanted to admit it openly, they got to each other in a very basic way. Just as they had years ago. Pretending that they didn't strike sparks was only going to make it worse.

"You're not sure at all," he corrected her softly as he kicked the toes of his shoes against the sill to knock the snow off.

"What do you mean—I'm not sure at all?" She stepped back to let him inside.

"I mean that I know why I'm trying like hell to pretend there's no chemistry between us." He switched the notebook from hand to hand as he shrugged out of his coat and hung it on the rack. "I'm trying to concentrate on my son. Why are you pretending?"

THREE

"I'm not pretending anything." She pushed her sweat-shirt sleeves up her forearms as if preparing to do battle.

"Careful, Taylor. You never could fool me. Besides, I aced chemistry in high school, college, and real life. I know what it feels like, even if you don't."

"Of course I know what chemistry feels like! But you can't possibly be serious. You've been almost a brother to me. Chemistry!" Taylor scoffed as she led the way into the living room. "If I didn't know better, I'd accuse you of hitting the spiked eggnog."

Drew knew a knee-jerk defensive reaction when he saw one, and he'd just witnessed a beaut. It only made him more curious about her reasons for ignoring the attraction between them. "I'm sorry to disappoint you, Mouse, but I am not your brother, and I haven't had any eggnog this morning, spiked or otherwise."

"Then would you like some?" she asked without missing a beat, and reversed directions to detour toward the kitchen.

"Whoa, Taylor," he ordered, blocking her path by placing his outstretched arm in her way. His hand rested lightly on her shoulder, and he used his leverage to angle her toward him. "I don't want eggnog. At least not this minute. I want an answer. What is it about me that has you running for cover? Every time I get within a foot of you, you look ready to bolt."

His fingers exerted an exploratory pressure along the rounded slope of her shoulder. "Like now. You're as tense as a department store manager trying to sober up Santa. What are you afraid is going to happen?"

"Nothing's going to happen." She flicked a glance at her shoulder and then back at his face. Her expression was one of determination, but her eyes reflected an uncertainty which belied her brave words. "Nothing."

"Not unless you want it to happen." Drew dropped his hand, but slowly. He was beginning to take this personally. Masculine pride urged him to show her just how easily he could make her want something to happen.

"Well, I don't want."

"Is it the age difference?"

"Of course that's not the reason!" she snapped in frustration, and then ground her teeth as she realized her mistake.

"Then why don't you tell me the real reason?" he drawled. His voice sounded like the purr of a cat who had a mouse neatly cornered, and the satisfied expression in his dark eyes was punctuated by one slightly raised brow.

She pushed her sleeves up again. "What difference does it make?"

"Well now, I won't know until I hear the reason."

"This is a stupid conversation." Taylor brushed past him and into the living room. Instead of turning to see if he followed, she dropped to her knees beside a large cardboard box, which was labeled "outdoor lights" in black Magic Marker. As she opened the flaps, she added, "Besides, you already said that you're supposed to be concentrating on your son."

"I'm supposed to be," he agreed with a sigh, "but you keep distracting me." He was right behind her, and Taylor could feel his gaze on her, as if he were waiting for something.

Probably the bell, Taylor thought, considering the fact their conversation was more like a prizefight. Drew had waded right in, throwing punch after punch. She had danced and dodged, but not quickly enough. Right now they were both in their corners considering strategy. She decided to come out swinging.

"Take a look around, Drew." She indicated the topsy-turvy state of the house by holding her arms wide. "Can't we both just agree that this is not the right time for this sort of thing?"

Laughing, he came around in front of her and parked himself in a wing chair that looked much too delicate to support his large frame. He considered her for a minute, softly tapping his notebook against his outstretched thigh. "What sort of 'thing' are we talking about here?"

"*Any* sort of thing," she clarified sharply as she lifted

a string of lights from the box. She plugged the end into an extension cord she had pulled out from beneath a lace-covered table, nodding when all the bulbs lit up in clear, rich blues, greens, yellows, reds, and oranges.

As she efficiently reached for the next string of lights, Drew leaned forward and asked, "If we agree that the attraction exists but that our lives are too complicated right now to pursue that attraction, does that mean you're going to stop jumping every time you see me or I accidentally touch you?"

"Does that mean you're going to stop 'accidentally' touching me?"

"I can promise that about as easily as you can promise not to keep me up at night."

Taylor's hand stilled, resting on the edge of the carton. Her concentration focused on what looked like miles of coiled green snakes. "I thought you were teasing about that."

"Not hardly."

She looked up then as if caught by an idea. "Why are you here, Drew?"

"You said I could come over and ask you questions anytime."

"I meant Christmas questions!"

"Oh, I know." He gave her a devilish grin and held up the notebook. "I didn't want to take up too much of your time, so I stayed up last night making a list."

Her blue eyes narrowed. "Making a list is what kept you up thinking about me?"

"While the lights were on, I was making a list. But then I put the pad down and turned the lights off.

Funny thing happened in the dark, Mouse. I was still thinking about you, but Christmas completely slipped my mind."

Taylor sucked in a breath of surprise. The thought of Drew lying in the dark, thinking of her, just her, was seductive. The fire in her cheeks alerted her to the blush which Drew seemed to find amusing. Scowling at him, she said, "I thought we agreed not to bring up this sort of thing."

"I agreed not to touch you. Besides, I didn't bring it up. You did. You wanted to know what kept me awake."

"All right. That's it. I admit defeat. You are much better at this little game of words than me." She got up from the floor. "So I'm going to sit on the couch; you ask me your questions and then go home where you belong."

She transferred a candy cane wreath, which sat on one end of the gold brocade couch, to the floor. When she pushed her hair back, she came away with the piece of tinsel and gave him a sour look. "Oh, thanks for telling me!"

"I thought it was cute."

"Cute." She rolled her eyes as she sank onto the couch cushion. Once she crossed her legs and her arms, Taylor said, "Ask."

Drew studied her body language as he made a show of flipping open his notebook. Her crossed limbs said a lot about how much distance she wanted between them. Too bad it was a wasted effort. If she'd asked, Drew could've told her that all the body language in the world wasn't going to change the fact that they were unfinished business, a question mark from the past that had never been answered, might never be answered. He'd also tell her that sometimes the pull of the past was too strong to resist. He was beginning to come to that conclusion himself.

"Okay. First question. Noah won't tell me what he wants from Santa Claus. All he'll say is that 'Santa knows.' So how do I find out?"

A grin tugged at the edge of Taylor's mouth. The man really was a babe in the woods when it came to kids and Christmas. "Sometimes you don't find out. It's part of being a parent. You listen. You bribe the elf at Santa's Castle, which they have in that collection of shops that passes for a mall over in Morriston. You try and get Noah to write a letter to Santa. You give Noah a toy catalogue and a pen for circling toys. If none of that works, then you guess. If you're lucky you'll get it right."

"Good plans. I was considering Chinese water torture."

She chuckled. "Save that for something really important, like pinning him down on a college when he's applied and been accepted at twenty schools."

"Got it. Okay, how big a tree do I get?"

"Since you don't have any ornaments, you should resist the urge to get a big, showy tree and stuff it with ornaments. Noah's little; even a small tree will look big to him. That way you can add more ornaments each year. A few at a time. Ones that will mean something to you and Noah."

"Is that what you did?"

The expression on Taylor's face softened. "That's what my mom did, and I kept up the tradition." She pointed at boxes stacked in a corner that were labeled "Clay," "Taylor," "David," "Jason," and "Mike." "She wanted all her children to take their memories with them when they got married and started their own families. Each year she bought a new ornament for each of us. Something special. Bo and Tim have already taken their boxes. Clay's will go home with him this year."

"How do you keep them straight?"

"Easy. Each kid has to put his own ornaments on the tree and take them off. You have as many ornaments as you are years old. Take 'em off, count 'em up, and you're done. When we were little, Momma helped." She drew her knees up and wrapped her arms around them, losing herself in the memories of childhood.

"The year my mother died, she bought a crystal star, the kind that goes on top of the tree." She looked up to be sure he knew the kind she meant. Drew nodded, so she continued, "She wrapped it up with my name and put it with the decorations because she knew she wasn't . . . she didn't have the strength to make it until Christmas. I didn't know about the star until I got out my box. When I opened it, there was a note. She told me not to worry, that she loved me, and that I could always find her if I just looked up."

Tears welled in her eyes, but didn't spill over. For that, Taylor was grateful. She gave Drew a weak smile. "The stars and I are old friends, although we don't chat as much as we used to when the boys were young."

In that moment, Drew stopped kidding himself

about his ability to walk away from Taylor. With the exception of Noah, Drew had never wanted to protect another human being more. She tugged at him in ways that were instinctive, ways he couldn't begin to define. Just as she had the day after the funeral when comfort had turned into something more. Something unforgettable. Something he'd thought was unforgivable.

"Well! Enough of that," Taylor declared, wiping her eyes. "I always get sentimental about Christmas. I promise not to do it again."

"Don't," he said roughly. He didn't like the idea of Taylor censoring her emotions for his benefit. He'd had too much of that growing up and in his marriage. "Don't promise."

"What? You like your women weepy?"

"I like my women honest."

Startled by the unexpected frankness of his answer, she looked away from his gaze. Unfolding her legs, Taylor got up and went back to the box of lights. "The way you say that makes me think that honesty has been a problem in your life."

"There's been little enough emotional honesty for me to want to hold on to it when I find it. At my house we didn't admit to emotions. What I learned about real families, I've learned in this house."

Taylor blanched. "Good Lord, we fight like cats and dogs. Just yesterday I admitted to wanting to murder my brothers."

"But you didn't."

"Of course not. I love them."

"Bingo."

Frowning, Taylor lifted the last two strands of lights out of the box. She made a show of untangling the cords to give herself time before she replied. The implication of his comment was staggering. "Are you saying your family doesn't love each other?"

Drew tossed his notebook on the end table and got up. He paced the room and threaded his fingers through his hair at the back of his neck. He stopped in front of the triple window which looked out onto the imperfect blanket of white created by yesterday's scant snowfall. At first glance, the world looked pretty, sparkling, but a second glance caught the bare spots, the places where the snow was nothing more than a thin veneer of ice.

The patchy whiteness reminded him of his childhood, of the frustration he felt knowing what he wanted but not how to get it. His parents weren't cruel. They just weren't loving. They attended to civic duty before family duty. When he finally spoke, he didn't turn away from the window. He shoved his hands in his pockets and shot straight from the hip.

"If you're asking me if my parents love me the way I love Noah, then the answer is no. They kept me warm and patted me on the head like a puppy, but that was about the extent of their tender loving care." He shrugged without turning away from the window. "That's why this Christmas is so important to me. I want more for Noah than I had. I've already lost five years I'll never get back. Sometimes I wonder if I can ever make it up. More often I wonder if I'm dad material. Having a child trust you is the scariest thing in the world."

Watching the squared shoulders, Taylor understood the burden he was carrying. It was the same one she had carried for too many years. She had a good idea what he was trying to find as he stared out the window—some sort of sign or a guarantee that everything would turn out all right in the end. She wished she could give it to him, but she couldn't. No one could.

Softly she said, "It's also the most wonderful thing in the world, having that little tiny hand nestled in yours. Kids think you can protect them against anything. Answer any question."

"Ah, yes, the questions. That brings up another problem," he grumbled, and turned around. "How do you answer those questions?"

"Like what?"

"Like—why didn't God fold up all of Arkansas?"

"Fold?"

"The mountains. We drove here from Arizona. When we left the Ozarks, Noah noticed the flat parts of the state and was very disappointed."

She giggled. "This I have to hear. Why didn't God fold up all of Arkansas?"

"Beats hell out of me." Drew came around the edge of the sofa and sat down again. "I was still reeling from the question before."

"I'm afraid to ask what that one was."

"He wanted to know if water was *invented* when I was young."

Taylor laughed so hard, she had to cover her mouth.

When she recovered, she made a show of critically looking him over from head to toe. "You don't look a day older than the wheel to me."

"Is that supposed to make me feel better?"

"It didn't?" She widened her eyes to what she hoped were round blue pools of innocence.

"Not hardly."

"You're not really feeling old?" she asked suddenly, remembering that he'd asked her about age once already today.

"Not old. More like two steps behind the rest of the world. Like I'm getting a late start."

Yet another point they had in common, Taylor discovered unhappily. They both felt like they were getting a late start on the life they wanted. Taylor was beginning to realize how dangerous it would be to spend much time in Drew's company. She understood him too well. She could fall for him too easily.

"Better late than never," she told him as she lifted all the lights back into the box and prepared to drag it toward the hallway.

"Here, I'll do that."

More quickly than she would have thought possible, Drew was kneeling beside her. For an instant they were shoulder to shoulder. His big hands lingered on hers before he brushed them away from the box. He caught and held her eyes with a gaze that warmed her all the way through and sabotaged her balance. She found herself leaning into a kiss that seemed inevitable.

"Where do you want it?" he asked, his words bringing her down to earth with stunning force as soon as she realized he meant the box, not the kiss.

"In—in the hallway, next to the coatrack. I'll get one of the boys to put them up after church."

Effortlessly he scooped up the unwieldy box. While he deposited the box where he was told, she pulled at the front of her sweatshirt to fan herself and tried to rationalize her response to his nearness. She hadn't been out on a real, get-a-kiss-at-the-end date in a long time. Yeah, that's the problem, she assured herself. She had simply mistaken Drew's intention. She was out of practice at fielding bedroom looks. With a mental sigh she admitted she was out of practice with quite a few men-related activities.

All of which meant that she'd better stay as far away from Drew as possible.

"What's next?" Drew asked and stopped just inside the archway. His hands were on his hips, and a lock of his thick hair had fallen across his forehead. He looked both too good and too good to be true. He looked like someone fighting for truth, justice, and the American way.

Unable to stop a grin, she asked, "Who do you think you are? Superman?"

Drew wasn't sure how to take her comment until he realized that his legs were braced apart, his hands were on his hips, and he'd just manhandled a heavy box. Taylor was closer to the mark than she realized, because it took superhuman effort to back away from the invitation she'd given him. The attraction they kept trying to ignore had blindsided him, whooshing through him like a brush fire. Common sense had kicked in just in time to keep him from ruining the fragile friendship that was developing between them.

He ran his fingers through his hair to comb the errant lock back in place. "Sorry to disappoint you, ma'am," he drawled, "but Noah's the real Superman, and he has the pajamas to prove it."

Thankful he wasn't going to make a big deal out of the almost kiss, she gave him a little free advice. "If I were you, I'd start looking right now for another set of those pj's in the next size up. Otherwise, Noah's going to be wearing this set forever."

"He can't wear them forever. They'll be too small."

Taylor gave a small pitying laugh. "You have a lot to learn about little boys, Hayseed. Trust me. He will wear them until you drag them from his tiny little clutches and burn them. By that time, the sleeves will only make it just past his elbows and three inches of his tummy will be showing in the space between the tops and the bottoms. The Velcro cape will have to be pinned on, and even worse, you will have taken the scissors and cut a slit in the neck so he can get the shirt on over his head. You'll be desperate to find some more pj's, but they'll be out of style or just plain hard to find."

"I'll make a note."

"You do that. It's good advice."

"I believe you."

"Then why aren't you writing it down?"

"Because Noah wears them all the time. I'll remember your advice every time I see him. Believe me,

Mouse, I listen very carefully to everything you say. Every word. I take you . . . very seriously."

"Oh." Taylor wasn't sure she wanted to be taken seriously by Drew. He made serious sound sensual. "If you want to get serious, shouldn't we get back to your Christmas questions?"

Before he could answer her, chaos returned to the Bishop household. The sound of car doors being slammed heralded the return of the clan. Taylor groaned. "They're early. I'll bet Martha talked them into coming home instead of going out for lunch. Damn!"

"Problem?"

"Only if you like peace and quiet. If I were you, I'd grab your notebook and make a run for it."

"I don't think so. Now . . . I'd be happy to grab you and make a run for it."

"Don't tempt me," Taylor mumbled under her breath as the front door opened and the sound of six people talking at once spilled in with the cold.

"No way, Dad. The Razorbacks aren't looking for another tailback," Jason said with all the authority of a college student privy to gossip on the university campus. "They're four deep in that spot as it is."

"Then you tell me why the assistant coach came to see Ronald Aubrey play? Not once but twice." Her father sounded smug.

"Clay, don't track snow inside," Martha said quickly. "Taylor and I have enough to do without cleaning up snow."

"Did anybody find out if Mrs. Austin used to be an

antiques dealer?" David asked. "I heard that some-where. If she is, I think we could use her advice."

"Do you have to have a college degree to be a pi-lot?" Mikey asked as he brought up the rear.

Drew, with amusement, and Taylor, with apprehen-sion, waited as the coats were shed and hung up, con-versation continuing among the group unabated. When Martha saw the box of lights, she wondered aloud, "Do you think Taylor checked them?"

"She always does, honey. I keep telling you—" Clay broke off as he caught sight of Drew. "Well, I'll be! You look great, man. Just great! How long have you been waiting for us?"

Taylor was momentarily forgotten as the family said hello to Drew. He and Clay did the requisite male greeting, which consisted of a one-second hug and a thump on the back. Her dad shook hands, and the boys just clapped him on the back and said, "Hey man!"

The scene should have been familiar, but it wasn't. Growing up, she'd spent her time looking at Drew. Now she found herself comparing him to her dad. Fa-thers didn't look like Drew when she was growing up. Fathers were supposed to be old and settled like her dad, who wore cardigan sweaters and brown wingtips with everything, not young and sexy like Drew, who wore pleated trousers that called attention to his flat abdomen.

Next came the nagging reminder that neither Drew nor she was exactly young. That much was obvious when she looked at her baby brothers and then at Drew. They were immature; he was experienced.

Last, she compared him to Clay. Both of them were tall and dark-eyed and loved to tease her, but Clay never made her pulse race. Never made her forget what she wanted to say. And never made her want to break her rules about becoming involved with family men. Clay was a brother, and that was one role that Drew had never come close to filling for her.

"Can you stay for lunch?" Martha asked, herding everyone toward the family room. "Taylor and I were about to whip up some soup and sandwiches."

Taylor did a double take at the pronouncement. "Martha, I've got all this Christmas stuff to unpack."

Martha waved away the excuse. "I'll help you after lunch. So, Drew, can you stay? Clay says you were his best friend in college. You have to stay."

Drew shook his head and stepped back out of the hallway. "No. I've got a few more questions for Taylor, and then I've got to head home."

"What kind of questions?" Martha asked him, much too interested for Taylor's peace of mind.

"She promised to set me straight on the finer points of the holiday."

"Why would she need to set you straight?" her sister-in-law asked as she looked back and forth between the two of them.

Drew began to explain about getting his son for Christmas, and Taylor began to feel trapped. All the guilt she felt at turning him down the first time came back. Along with the guilt came an uneasy feeling of impending doom. Drew's version of the events was completely accurate and managed to make her sound like a hard-hearted Hannah.

"You turned this man down!" Martha gasped, and whirled to face her. "Taylor, how could you?"

"How could I?" she asked incredulously. She shouldn't have let her temper get the best of her, but she did. "How could I turn him down? How could I say yes! Someone has to put our holiday together!"

Unexpectedly, Martha laughed and put her arm through Clay's. "Is that all you're worried about, honey? I can hold down the fort here. You don't have to do a thing this year, except your own shopping and helpin' old Drew here make a little boy happy."

Just as she was about to protest, her own father painted her into a corner. "She's right, you know. You deserve a break, and playing Santa to a little boy has got to be a lot more fun than catering to this bunch. You go ahead if you want to, Taylor. We'll get by. This is supposed to be your vacation."

Silently Drew surveyed the scene in front of him. He wanted nothing more than to have Taylor's help, but he knew a lot more about her than he did yesterday. He knew that Taylor's reasons for shying away from him and Noah were a lot more complicated than decorating the Bishop house.

Clay and his wife looked mighty pleased with themselves, as if they'd planned the whole thing all along. Coach Bishop looked worried. Taylor looked uncertain. When she looked at him, he thought he saw a touch of panic. Poor Taylor, she thought she was being thrown to the wolves. Wolf, he corrected. And he was going to do his best to catch her.

"I think you people are foolish to let her go, but if you don't need her, Noah and I certainly do. How about it, Taylor? Will you help me?"

FOUR

Everyone's eyes were on her. She could feel their expectation as if it were a tangible quality. But her attention was on Drew, on the promise in his eyes, a promise he couldn't even know she needed, one she shouldn't believe but did—a promise that he'd help her find the magic again. All she had to do was say yes.

In the space of a few seconds she mentally turned the situation every which way but loose. There was risk in saying yes and risk in saying no. She didn't want this choice. Hadn't asked for this choice, but that didn't seem to matter in the grand scheme of her life. For better or worse, guilt always took a hand in the decision making; guilt had shaped her future for so long, she was beginning to get used to it.

Dredging up a smile, she turned to Martha and warned, "You don't know what you're volunteering for."

Martha flashed a grin of brilliant white teeth and

gave Clay's arm a little squeeze, as if celebrating a victory. "It's just Christmas. We'll manage."

Just Christmas? She bit her tongue and faced her dad. "Are you sure? I mean—" Taylor floundered for a moment. "The boys. Christmas has always—"

"Taylor Marie, the boys are grown. They won't even notice you're gone. They'll probably con Martha into putting their ornaments on the tree for them." He moved closer and clasped her shoulder briefly as he gave her a wink. "Why don't you see what you can do for Drew." With that, he ambled toward the family room and the noise of a pro football game that Mikey, Jason, and David were watching on television.

"Well," Taylor said heavily, realizing she'd run out of excuses. "I guess that settles it."

"I guess it does," Drew agreed, with only a trace of triumph in his voice. "Would asking you to come over right now be pushing my luck?"

"Of course not," Martha answered for her. "Clay, grab their coats. Taylor, you go on out with Drew and have some fun."

"Drew isn't asking for a date," she said sharply. Her sister-in-law was really beginning to get on her nerves with this mother-hen routine. "Besides, I have to finish—"

"The only thing you have to do is go off with Drew and have a good time." Martha lowered her voice so only Taylor could hear. "It may not be a date, but he's unattached and gorgeous. Now scat before I have to get really obvious about this matchmaking stuff!"

With not-so-subtle pressure, Martha maneuvered

them toward the door, and Clay handed them their coats. Never once did Martha's perfect smile waver. Never once did she give Taylor the slightest opportunity to object as she pushed her out the door. Clay performed the same service for Drew. For the second time in two days, Taylor found herself on the porch and thinking murderous thoughts. Only this time she included Martha in the mayhem she was contemplating.

As if he could read the thoughts running through her mind, a chuckle escaped Drew, but he cut the sound off instantly when she swung around to glare at him. In fact, he was the picture of innocence, but she wasn't fooled. Not one bit. He had the look of a man biding his time, very sure of getting what he wanted.

"This isn't funny, Hayseed."

"What do you want me to do? Cringe and look embarrassed because I won this round? I don't think so, darlin'. I'm not going to lie and say that this isn't exactly what I wanted." As he adjusted the fit of his coat across his shoulders, he looked too rugged for her peace of mind.

"You don't fight fair."

"Maybe not. Maybe telling my sad tale in front of your new sister-in-law was hitting below the belt, but it worked. They've had you for years, and they obviously don't appreciate you. I do. I want you with me and Noah for Christmas, and I'll take you any way I can get you."

Then he sincerely thanked her for offering to help, told her that black Jeep was his, and waited for her to precede him down the steps. On the way to the vehicle,

Taylor decided a confident winner was worse than a bad loser. Particularly when the winner had a way of making her think about all sorts of games that a man and a woman could play, games where losing was winning and both players ended up breathless and hot.

The drive to Drew's house was mercifully short. Taylor sat as close to the door as possible and told herself repeatedly that the fluttery sensation in her stomach didn't mean a thing. She was *not* looking forward to being alone with Drew. She was *not* glad Martha had forced her into this. She couldn't be glad, because that would be foolishly asking for trouble, and Taylor knew all about trouble. It was sitting on the other side of the Jeep, looking satisfied and sexy.

The smart course was to see this as a job, an event like those she planned every day in her position as event coordinator for the Hope Foundation, the charitable organization that served as a clearinghouse of funds for dozens of worthy causes. *Worthy causes.* Now there was a phrase that summed up her feelings exactly. Drew and Noah were just another worthy cause, she told herself, pleased that she'd been able to put a new spin on the circumstances.

With any luck at all, Noah would take an instant dislike to her. Then she wouldn't have to worry about liking him in return. Besides, she wasn't going to be around long enough to worry about becoming attached to Noah or his father. She intended to whip this Christmas together in record time. She'd help buy the tree and some decorations, write down a few recipes, pick out some Christmas music, maybe take them to see the

Enchanted Glade at Wills' Department Store in Morriston, but then she'd be gone.

Nope, this wouldn't take long at all, because Drew and Noah didn't have dozens of traditions that had to be observed every year. Yep, before Martha could hang the outdoor lights on the wrong trees, she'd be home where she belonged, where it was safe. She was actually smiling when Drew pulled up in his driveway.

His street was the oldest in town, presided over by towering oak trees older than any living resident of Harvey. The white antebellum-style home had actually been built after the war by a carpetbagger who had seen a chance to buy himself a bit of respectability. When Taylor was fifteen, the Haywoods had bought the house from the carpetbagger's descendants. During that first fateful summer in Harvey, Drew and Clay discovered they were both juniors at the University of Arkansas; a friendship was born, and so was a crush that lasted for years.

The memory of her starry-eyed infatuation strengthened her determination to treat her unavoidable proximity to Drew in a businesslike manner. She unbuckled her seat belt and slid out of the all-but-new black Jeep, not bothering to wait for Drew. She wandered to the center of the front yard and took a good look around. She catalogued the size and shape of the pines, oaks, and magnolias; and the width of the house itself; and the neighbors' decorating schemes, which seemed to consist only of red bows on mailboxes.

Drew got out of the Jeep more slowly, joining her in the middle of the yard. The way she had rocketed out of the Jeep gave him a pretty good indication of how long she'd be around if he didn't find some way to slow her down. She was much too intent on getting the whole holiday thing over with. After he slowed her down, he needed to figure out why she was so wary of the attraction between them.

"So what do you think?" he asked. "Do I need to take out a loan?"

She smiled. "Not just yet. But starting from scratch means it won't be cheap."

"Don't worry about the money. This is an investment in Noah's future. Come on." He took her hand and led her toward the house. "I want you to meet him."

Taylor's eyes widened as a surge of awareness coursed through her at the casual contact. She hadn't bothered to put on her mittens for the short drive, so her bare palm slid against his, the friction warming her skin and unexpectedly making her senses hum in anticipation of more intimate touches. He adjusted and settled his grip with a tiny movement of his fingers and thumb that was as seductive as it was startling.

Her gaze focused on their joined hands, one still slightly tanned and one pale; one large and one small. The differences between them fascinated her, fascinated her too much. In that instant she was conscious of how long it had been since a man had seriously tempted her to pursue more than a friendship.

A tingle of foreboding slipped up her spine, and instinct warned her that there was nothing remotely casual about Drew's actions. The hand-holding was all part of his plan to make sure she didn't back out of the agreement. He wanted to make her aware of him as a man and sucker her into spending more time than she should at the Haywood house.

Damn the man! He was oh-so-cleverly baiting the hook, disguising flirtation as friendship.

If he didn't fight fair, how was she ever going to get through this? By laying down some ground rules, she answered herself. Focusing on the job and not the man should be a very simple solution to her problem. As they approached the double oak doors leading inside, she pulled her hand free and made a mental note to buy two large wreaths.

"Drew, I've already said I'll help. You don't have to keep up this touchy-feely stuff to make sure I won't change my mind."

He stopped abruptly with his hand on the door handle and turned a surprised expression on her. "I wasn't aware that taking the hand of a friend was considered touchy-feely."

Tilting her head, she considered him with a raised eyebrow. "Right."

"I'm perfectly serious. My personal definition of touchy-feely includes a helluva lot more than hand-holding." His gaze slid slowly down the length of her body and back up. His voice was warm and rumbled through her, shaking butterflies loose. "A helluva lot. Believe me, when I think about touching you, holding hands is not what comes to mind. It's not a bad place to start, but it's not where I finish."

Taylor's mouth went dry. Her tongue almost swiped

a trail across her bottom lip before she caught herself. She snapped her mouth shut and swallowed instead. Every second she spent with Drew reinforced the idea that he saw her as a desirable woman.

Lord, she was tempted to believe this fantasy, but she knew it was the past talking, the need to close the book on puppy love. She refused to give in to that need. She wanted to forget about the past and move on to the freedom of the future.

Winter's silence swirled around them like snow, building the tension as they faced off with Drew's blunt declaration suspended invisibly between them. Before Taylor could find her voice to remind him that he couldn't finish what she wasn't willing to start, a stylishly dressed woman in a burgundy skirt and sweater pulled open the door.

"Ah, Drew. I thought I heard a car." Her thick white hair was cut short and fluffed in windblown style. She was beautiful in a classic way and not nearly as old as the white hair and pearl choker hinted. She waved them hastily into the entranceway. "Why are you still standing out in the cold? It's supposed to snow again any minute."

If Drew was embarrassed to be caught standing in the cold instead of coming right inside, he gave no sign of it as he spoke. "Thanks, Roxie. I'd like you to meet Taylor Bishop. She's a friend who's going to be helping me with Christmas. Taylor, this is Mrs. Roxanne Penney, my next-door neighbor and my savior in the last couple of weeks since I moved home."

The woman smiled. "What he means is that I'm a

bored old woman who'd rather come play with Noah than sit at home counting my aches and pains."

"Nice to meet you, Mrs. Penney."

"Call me Roxie, dear. Everyone does. Even Noah. Makes me feel younger." Turning to Drew, she said, "I'll dash home now that you're here. Noah's coloring in the kitchen." She patted Drew's cheek in a consoling gesture as she passed him. "He didn't eat much at lunch."

"He never does."

"No, he doesn't." She sighed. "He's not a thing like my grandchildren. Call me if you need me."

After Roxie left, Taylor said, "Nice lady."

"That she is, one of the best. Don't know what I would have done without her." He shed his coat and took hers, laying them over the banister rather than putting them in the closet. "Someone should have told me that being a full-time parent is a lot like juggling machetes without any training."

A ghost of a smile touched Taylor's mouth as she studied his face, fascinated by the tiny cleft in his chin. Already she could see the beginnings of a five o'clock shadow across his jawline. "You must be doing okay. I don't see any nicks," she teased.

"Then you aren't close enough." His voice was low, suggestive; his reply an invitation.

He didn't move or hold his arms out, but it was an invitation to walk into them nonetheless. Quietly, with one simple statement, Drew had blown her tidy little holiday solution all to hell. Everything he said, everything he did, was going to be shaded with hidden meaning.

He wasn't going to cross the line, but he was going to walk right up to it, maybe even stand on it a little. Just as he had on the porch. He was putting her on notice. He had no intention of ignoring the heat simmering beneath the surface of their relationship, and he wasn't going to let her put distance between them.

She remembered seeing the same glint in his eyes years ago. When he wanted something, he planned carefully and waited patiently. Whether he wanted to win a game of Monopoly or finagle another slice of pie, he planned, and he waited, and he won. She'd seen him do it too often to ignore that glint, but right now she didn't have a clue as to how to answer the challenge without losing the game.

They were playing for more than control of Park Place and Boardwalk; they were playing for a monopoly of her time. Drew wanted more than his fair share, and he was willing to seduce her to get it. He wanted her to help him create traditions that would last; he wanted her to make memories for Noah. Both of which meant allowing herself to be a real part of their family for a while. She'd have to come to the Haywood house early and stay late.

She'd have to create her own memories in the process, and then when Christmas was over, she'd have to walk away from a small boy who'd already been abandoned once or risk falling in love and being tied down forever.

If she allowed Drew to seduce her, to make her care

about him and Noah, then she'd have no choice in the future. Guilt would take over and send her directly to jail, without passing Go. Fighting her attraction for Drew was the only hope she had of avoiding the no-win situation.

From less than a couple of feet away, he watched her and waited for her to roll the dice. Taylor silently cursed the patience in his dark eyes until an idea dawned. An absolutely brilliant idea. Every time Drew wanted to get close, all she had to do was put Noah right smack in his way. Like right now.

"Didn't you want me to meet Noah?"

At her innocent question, guilt flickered briefly in his eyes. He shot her a suspicious look, but the beauty of her plan was that he couldn't complain. The whole point of her being here was for Noah. "Yeah, I did. This way."

Drew blazed a trail to the kitchen, and Taylor followed, cataloguing her surroundings the same way she had catalogued the front yard. The ceiling was easily twelve feet. It was a shame that Drew didn't have enough ornaments for a big tree. She could imagine how the room would look with a huge spruce positioned right next to the tall front window. The lights would glow softly, spilling color out into the night.

When she stopped in front of the fireplace and its heavy wooden mantel, Drew said, "There's another fireplace in the kitchen. I wasn't sure where to hang Noah's stocking."

"Stockings—plural. You should hang one too."

"So you can put a lump of coal in it?" The corner of his mouth quirked upward.

"Actually, I was considering switches and ashes."

"You think that's fair? I haven't even been bad." Drew joined her by the fireplace and rested his forearm against the mantel, enjoying the way her eyes widened a tiny fraction. "Yet."

"Wanna bet?" she mumbled as she scooted away and pushed up her sleeves.

Drew wondered when she'd figure out that running away from little moments of intimacy wasn't going to make him go away. It only increased the tension between them by pulling the strings of attraction tighter. When she'd put enough space between them to make her comfortable, he made sure he had her full attention and then pushed up the sleeves of his cable-knit sweater to test a theory he had about Taylor Marie. Bull's-eye. She caught the significance of the deliberate gesture instantly.

"Something wrong, Mouse?"

"No. Nothing," she answered softly and quickly to cover the appalling realization that Drew Haywood could read her like a book.

Just great! Taylor thought. *This job is getting worse by the minute.* Somehow he knew pushing up her sleeves was a nervous habit. Every time he made her squirm, he'd know unless she instantly eradicated a lifelong habit. Fat chance of that happening. Especially when she had a feeling Drew would be spending a lot of time backing her into situations that called for sleeve pushing.

"About the stockings," she said in a rush, "the reason you should hang two is because nothing's more depressing than one lonely stocking. As for which mantel, always hang the stockings on the fireplace closest to the tree. But if you want, we can decorate the kitchen fireplace too. We just won't put stockings on it."

"Why not?"

"We don't want to confuse Santa or make him haul in any more lumps of coal than he absolutely has to."

"Taylor, darlin', you are the Emily Post of Christmas etiquette. See why we need you around here?"

She let him pass and continue toward the kitchen without commenting or correcting him. The real question was not whether they needed her, but whether she needed them. The answer was a very big no. She needed her own life, not theirs. Taylor Bishop wasn't anybody's mother. Not anymore.

When they got to the kitchen, Taylor stood paralyzed in the doorway, held there by memories of another little boy who had colored quietly at the kitchen table, on his knees in a straight-back chair, with a look of utter concentration on his face. Mikey had colored that way when he was little, just like Noah, with his rump sticking out as he hovered over his creation. Watching the little blond head and the way he pushed his bottom lip out and then sucked it back behind his front teeth was like getting a piece of Mikey's childhood back.

"Hiya, buddy!" Drew said softly. "I want you to meet a friend."

When his son looked up, all resemblance to Mikey

ended, and the breath caught in Taylor's chest. He was perhaps the most beautiful child she'd ever seen, but she knew why Drew was so worried. The little boy looked first at his daddy and then at her. Big gray eyes that should have been glinting silver with mischief and curiosity were guarded and shadowed. He put his crayon carefully away and slid down from the chair, letting one hand rest on the table. As if he needed an anchor.

Such a big little man, Taylor thought as she watched him. So controlled, so careful. He had on a spotless cream sweater and blue jeans with topsiders. She hated the way he stood so straight and looked so lost in his grown-up clothes. "Hello, Noah. I'm Taylor."

"Hi." He had the kind of voice that shouldn't belong to a child, the kind of voice that didn't know how to giggle. The silence grew as they looked at each other. For the first time, even Drew looked tense. Finally, taking a big breath obviously meant to screw up his courage, Noah whispered, "Daddy said you could help us fix Christmas."

An invisible hand gave Taylor's heart a good squeeze, and she wasn't sure what to say until he took one step forward, crossed his fingers, and added, "If it's all right with you, I want the Christmas like Daddy had. The one with the gingerbread men."

In that moment she stopped kidding herself about her clever plan to keep herself safe by writing down a few recipes and disappearing into the sunset. How could she? Noah's Christmas was more important than the little rules she lived her life by. She'd simply have to figure out how to give Noah his holiday and ignore her hormones. If she was careful, she could do this for a week, but she wouldn't give up the rest of her life. She wouldn't.

Taking a deep breath just as he had, she screwed up her courage. Taylor wiggled her eyebrows at the solemn child and grinned. "Just call me Doc Holiday, because I'm here to make sure you get a Christmas just like Daddy had, complete with gingerbread men."

Noah's eyes widened, but he didn't grin or shout or dance a happy little jig. He still hadn't uncrossed his fingers. "Can we get the tree now?"

"I don't see why not." Drew, relaxed again, reached out a hand to tousle his son's hair. Noah had to tilt his head all the way back to look up at his dad, who suggested, "Why don't you go upstairs and wash your face before we go?"

"Yes, sir." Noah walked between them, very careful not to bump into her, but he did cut his eyes up as he passed, his face full of worry.

Taylor winked at him and made a sudden decision as she stepped into the kitchen and out of his way. "Don't you fret, Noah. I'll be right here when you get back. And we're going to buy the biggest tree they've got. One that's so big the star is going to touch the ceiling."

The look of hope and delight on his son's face nearly did Drew in. His heart broke each time he had to face what Anna had done to Noah—turned him into a cautious little man who didn't trust people. Watching the exchange, Drew wondered what Noah would be like if someone half as warmhearted as Taylor had been his mother.

A smile darted briefly across Noah's face and then disappeared when he furrowed his brows. "Can we get some more of that berry stuff too?"

"Berry stuff?" Drew asked.

"Missy's toes." Noah pointed above the door.

Both adults looked up. Taped above the door, with only the tip extending below the header, was a tiny sprig of mistletoe tied with a thin red ribbon and sporting a few leathery green leaves and waxy white berries.

In the sad, judgmental manner that only a disappointed five-year-old can assume, Noah told them, "Doesn't look much like toes, but I said my 'thank you' to Roxie anyway, Daddy." He lowered his voice to a whisper as if trying to spare Roxie's feelings. "But I think we need a better one."

"That's *mistle*toe," Taylor explained, fighting a grin and refusing to look at Drew for fear of lapsing into laughter. "Not Missy's toes. We can get a bigger bunch, but are you sure you want some more? 'Cause if you get caught under the mistletoe by a girl she gets to *kiss* you!"

Laughing at Noah's horrified expression, Drew confirmed the worst, "That's right, buddy. It's a tradition."

When Noah looked blank, Taylor added, "A tradition is sort of a rule that's been handed down for hundreds of years."

Drew got closer to his son and warned, "You get caught under the mistletoe, and you're a goner. You have to stand there and take the kiss like a man."

"You mean it's a real rule?" He looked horrified again. "You have to let Taylor kiss you now?"

"Kiss me?" Drew glanced up and contemplated the plant above him. Sure enough, he'd shifted until he was directly beneath the thing. His position was pure coincidence, but he had every intention of taking advantage of his good luck. He pretended to sigh in resignation. "I guess so, buddy. A tradition should never be broken. I have to let her kiss me."

"I can't watch." Noah put his hands over his eyes, carefully spreading them so he could actually see if he wanted to.

Stunned, Taylor's mouth fell open. *Kiss Drew?* What she wanted to do was wipe that smirk off his face. Seconds ticked by as he stared her down, daring her to kiss him. Noah was blatantly peeking through his fingers now, waiting to see tradition translated into action. Not only did she have an audience, she had to make the kiss seem natural and not charged with the electricity spearing through the air. Just get it over with, she told herself, but didn't move.

Finally the thump of the furnace kicking into high gear snapped the tension. With lightning speed she stepped up to Drew, raised on her tiptoes, and pecked him on the cheek. "There! All done."

When it was over, little Noah seemed as relieved as she was and both let out long breaths at the same time. As he walked away, he mumbled to himself, "Wait till I tell Roxie. I don't think she knew 'bout this."

When he was out of earshot, Taylor turned on Drew, poking him in the chest with her finger and forcing him backward into the dining room. "Don't do that again."

"Do what?"

"Trick me into kissing you. I'm not interested in holiday romance. I thought I made that clear. If not, let me make it clear now."

"The little mistletoe story was yours, not mine." He flicked his gaze up at the mistletoe hanging directly above her head, then back down at her. "As I recall, mistletoe rules work both ways, Mouse. Noah's gone, and now it's my turn. But I want a real kiss."

Instinct told her to move, to sidestep the kiss, but a bittersweet memory held her frozen in place. She'd shared a real kiss with Drew once before, after her mother's funeral. She had felt so alone, so afraid to let anyone know that she was a fraud and only pretending to be strong. She remembered the way Drew watched her all afternoon after the funeral, as if he could see inside and understood. She closed her eyes against the reality of the memory as it washed over her.

Alone in the kitchen, she desperately tried to remember how to make a pot of coffee, but the fear that had paralyzed her all day made the simple task impossible. All she could think about were the promises she had made to her mother and about how much faith she had had in her daughter. Too much faith. Unshed tears already blurred her vision when she felt Drew behind her.

"Come here." He took the wadded coffee filter out of her hands and pulled her into his arms, cradling her head on his shoulder. "You don't have to pretend with me. It's okay."

Tears ran silently down her face as she looked up. "That's just it. You don't understand. It's never going to be okay again."

He kissed her then, a small reassuring kiss, but she wanted more. She wanted the heat of his kiss to make the cold inside her heart go away. So she opened her mouth beneath his. Never in her life had she experienced such raw emotions. It was almost an overload, but she didn't care. The fear was melting. Every part of her felt alive and safe.

Then the kiss was over, Drew was apologizing, and nothing was ever the same again.

"I won't apologize this time," Drew warned softly when her eyes snapped open. He'd been replaying the same memory—their only kiss, which had begun as comfort and turned into something totally unexpected. "You ought to know one thing before I kiss you, Taylor. I've given up pretending that Noah's the only reason I came to find you."

FIVE

"I don't believe you." It was a whisper, a defense. Not a very good one, Drew decided.

"Maybe you'll believe me when I kiss you. And I am going to kiss you, Taylor darlin'. With any luck, kissing a beautiful woman under the mistletoe will become the first Haywood holiday tradition."

"Careful what you wish for, you may not like what you get."

"I liked it before." He braced a hand on either side of the door.

"Then why—" she clamped her mouth shut on the revealing words.

"Because you were sixteen." He leaned in until his chest almost touched her breasts, but not quite. She could have stepped back, but she didn't. Her tongue touched the corner of her mouth as he continued, "What was I supposed to do? Take advantage of your confusion? I was older. Too old for you."

He brought his head down, beginning to slant it, willing her to understand. "Old enough to know that my responsibility was to protect you, not hurt you more by taking what I wanted when you were afraid of being alone."

Taylor's line of vision narrowed to encompass only his face, the intensity in his eyes, and the firm set of his jaw as he admitted feelings of guilt she never knew existed. The change in perspective did a funny thing to her heart. An old hurt eased up and in its place was compassion for Drew, who had had to choose for both of them that day. She knew all about making guilty choices.

"I didn't realize," she whispered, searching his eyes for the promise that had been there earlier, the one about the magic. She found it. Hesitantly she put a hand against his ribs and flattened her palm.

Drew wondered if the movement was to push him away, until she curled her fingers into his sweater. That was all the sign he needed. "You're not sixteen anymore, and this time"—his lips brushed against hers quickly, roughly—"I'm going to finish what I start. Open your mouth, Taylor."

Instinct obeyed a second before logic objected, and it was too late for her to back away. Drew's mouth came down on hers, and she was lost. There was nothing of comfort in this kiss, just need—past, present, hers, his. She anchored her hands in his sweater, clinging to the odd combination of soft and rough sensations beneath her fingers, sensations that mirrored the feel of his tongue twined with hers. She felt safe and alive. She gave herself up to those feelings.

Drew sensed Taylor's surrender, felt her soften, and heard a tiny sound that might have been a sigh. Kissing her was like coming in out of the cold. She warmed his soul and kindled a fire in his belly. He wanted more, but he was bound by the same trust she gave him years ago. He couldn't abuse her gift by taking more than a kiss.

When the rounded contours of her body pressed intimately into his, he tightened his grip on the door facing rather than let his hands roam over her soft curves. Every second was heaven and hell. He wanted to slide his hands down her back and cup her rump, which he knew would feel so soft and round and as if it were made for his touch.

Slowly his grip on the jamb loosened. He was seconds away from breaking his promise to himself when he heard footsteps in the upstairs hallway. Taylor must have heard them too, because her hands stilled against his rib cage a second before she broke the kiss, quickly stepping back. Despite the fact that she'd given as good as she got during the kiss, her eyes were worried, uncertain. She had "I've made a mistake" written all over her.

Taking a resigned breath, Drew cursed silently.

Taylor closed her eyes and tried to get her bearings. The man hadn't laid a hand on her and her pulse was galloping. There wasn't enough air in the room, and her hands felt empty. Parts of her that hadn't been heard from in ages were frustrated. Why did Drew have to rattle all those secret places? Why couldn't he have been some nice, unmarried, Wal-Mart assistant manager whose family lived in Alaska?

"Am I so hard to look at?" Drew asked quietly, cutting across her thoughts and reminding her that her eyes were still closed. By putting his hands low on his hips and spreading his fingers across his abdomen, he drew her attention to the sweater, which her hands had pulled and stretched so that it sagged in front.

"Well?" he asked, impatient. "Am I that hard to look at?"

When she didn't respond, Drew released an exasperated sigh. "A simple question, Taylor. All I require is a simple answer."

But there wasn't a simple answer. The words were all mixed up with emotions she'd been hoping to avoid. Physically, Drew Haywood was easy on the eyes, but he was hell on her emotions. Looking at him wouldn't be hard at all if he'd just focus those incredible eyes, which were more sinful and two shades darker than chocolate, somewhere over her shoulder instead of on her mouth, her body. He jumbled up her priorities. He looked hungry for more than she was willing to give. And he wanted an answer.

How could she tell him that she didn't have one because she couldn't think when he stared at her? How could she explain that it wasn't the package but what was inside? How could she say, "I'm sorry, but a man like you wants kids and PTA meetings and that makes you the bad guy."

She escaped having to answer because Noah reached the foot of the stairs and called to his dad. His raised voice was a froggy monotone. "Do I have to put on the red rubber boots?"

"I think so. Where we're going is liable to be wet and muddy," Drew answered without turning his head. He knew he wouldn't need to. His son didn't argue. he never did, but his footsteps going up the stairs were noticeably heavier than when he had descended. A month ago they wouldn't have been.

When the sound faded, Drew told her, "We've got maybe five minutes while he puts on the boots." He held up his hands, making the same gesture a street fighter makes when motioning an opponent to come on. "Say it, Taylor. Let's get this over with."

"Get what over with?"

He controlled his temper by pivoting and taking a few steps along the outer edge of the oriental rug beneath the dining room table. "Don't play games, Mouse. You never could fool me. We both know that right now you're trying to settle on the best way to tell me the kiss was a mistake."

"It was." She was absolutely certain of that. "Don't do it again."

"Why? I enjoyed it. And correct me if I'm wrong . . ." He paused in mock hesitancy, but the half smile on his face was confident, knowing. "I'm pretty sure you enjoyed it too."

"That's beside the point," she snapped.

"No, that is the point, Taylor. You enjoyed it."

"Well, I didn't want to!"

"So tell me why!" Each word was bitten off like an order. "Is it me in particular or men in general?"

"What difference does it make?" She pushed her sleeves up.

"You're squirming, Mouse. I guess it must be me."

"Oh, for God's sake!" Taylor folded her arms across her midriff. Now he looked hurt. "It's nothing personal."

"Nothing *personal*?" Drew scoffed and looked even more offended.

"Of course not." She told the first plausible lie that came to mind. "My job's pretty demanding. Which means I don't have much time for a social life, so I don't date out of Little Rock. Too many complications. You know how it is when you try to hold a relationship together over the telephone."

"No, I don't. Do you?"

She opened her mouth, but nothing came out.

"Didn't think so. Then I guess I'll just have to show you how creative a guy and a telephone can be."

"No! That won't be necessary. I mean . . ." She faltered and quit trying to explain, because she had no idea what she meant or how to get out of the hole she'd dug for herself.

Drew began to feel better now that he had a handle on her reluctance. Fear of long-distance relationships was something he could overcome. "Trust me, Taylor. You, me, and a telephone—this could work. You still have that pink Princess phone in your bedroom? The one your Dad gave you when you turned sixteen?"

"No." But she did.

"Liar." Drew laughed and headed for his study. "I bet if I look in the phone book, I'll find your dad never disconnected that extra children's line. The one you were so proud of. The one that rang in your bedroom."

"All right. All right!" Her admission stopped him in the center of the living room. "The phone's still there. I don't know about the phone line."

"Don't worry. That's a mystery easily solved by looking in the phone book."

Almost afraid, she asked, "And what if it is?"

"Then you can expect a call."

"You don't fight fair, Hayseed."

"I never will. Not when I'm fighting for something I want."

Before she could argue that he was fighting for a lost cause, Noah clumped down the stairs, stopping at the bottom and waiting expectantly. "I'm ready."

"So am I, buddy. So am I." Drew grinned at Taylor.

The Boy Scout lot was set up on a vacant parcel of land that had been a gas station until the owner ended up on the wrong side of the IRS. Following bankruptcy, the station was pulled down and the tanks dug up. The nice-sized corner lot was now the site of a major Scout fund-raiser every year, the profits sending a fair number of boys to camp. A sandwich-type sign sat on the corner, emblazoned with the words CHRISTMAS TREE LANE and TROOP 487.

Along each side of the tract, ordinary lightbulbs were strung like Christmas lights between makeshift poles, ready to illuminate the night. Drew had no trouble imagining what the lot would look like tonight, lit up and fragrant, an evergreen oasis in the snow. He wondered if the workers ever got tired of the pine scent that filled the air.

Inside the makeshift boundary, the remaining Scotch pines, firs, and spruces were neatly arranged in meager rows. Two empty metal folding chairs were positioned at the "entrance." A couple of Scouts shuffled their feet to keep them warm while an adult volunteer looked on from his position behind the roughly made counter, a plank and two barrels, on which wreaths and greenery were piled.

Drew coasted up to the edge of the curb and killed the engine. "Okay troops, we're here."

In unison, they all unbuckled their seat belts. Noah scooted to the edge of his seat and stared. "They don't have very many."

"That's all right," Taylor told him as she opened the door and slid out. "They still have ours."

Taylor froze. *Ours? They still have ours?* She couldn't believe her ears. How could she have said something like that? The word 'ours' implied she was part of the family. She knew better than to think in family terms, much less say them out loud. She wanted to take it back, but that was impossible. Doing so would only advertise her real objection to Drew and start another round of questions.

Surreptitiously she glanced over at him to see if he had noticed her slip of the tongue. Apparently he hadn't, because he was grinning and waiting for Noah to hop out of the Jeep and into his arms. That he loved his son was obvious, painfully obvious. The two of them belonged together, but they looked nothing alike.

With his blond hair and gray eyes, Noah looked more like her son than Drew's. Moments like this forced her to acknowledge the ticking of her biological clock and the alarm that was increasingly difficult to ignore. When she lay down to sleep that night, no doubt she'd toss and turn, plagued by recurring doubts about the wisdom of her choice to remain single and childless.

"Which one is ours?" Noah asked as he slid to the ground and tried to match his dad stride for stride. "And how come you don't have to wear boots?"

"Because I don't accidentally-on-purpose end up in the middle of every puddle in the neighborhood. And our tree is the one Taylor picks out."

Noah let his dad walk on, but he waited for Taylor. "Can I help?"

"Help me? I'm here to help you. I give advice—hints—and you pick out the tree."

"All by myself?" He waved her downward, closer. "What if I pick the wrong one?"

"That's impossible."

With a hand on his shoulder, she steered him past the Scouts, to whom she gave a smile and a shake of her head. For this first trip, she wanted Noah to roam without anyone hovering around and hurrying his selection. "The tree we're looking for is perfect. You'll know it when you see it."

"How?"

"Because it will look exactly the way you want your

Christmas tree to look. Some people like 'em skinny, some like 'em bushy. Others want their tree to be shaped in a perfect triangle, and some people want their tree to have character—like a crooked trunk or two points at the top."

"Which ones do you like?"

Taylor had to chuckle. "I'm a sucker for character. I always seem to take home the tree no one else wants."

"Do you still love it like a good tree? Just like it was the best tree ever?"

The unexpected question brought Taylor to an abrupt halt. She was at a loss for an answer until she realized Noah was asking not about the trees but about himself. In a roundabout way, he was asking if little boys who weren't wanted could ever be loved again. At that moment, if she could have gotten her hands around Anna's neck, she would gladly have strangled the woman. She understood the controlled anger in Drew's voice when he talked about his ex-wife.

Noah looked up at her, waiting and quiet. That's when she remembered Drew's comment about a child's trust being the scariest thing in the world. This was a face that would have scared him to death, so grave, so earnest.

Lightly, she touched her index finger to Noah's cold, red nose. "I always love it just like it's the best tree ever. Because it's my tree and nobody else's."

Noah rewarded her with a rare smile, which she returned.

"Of course," she warned, "there's more to this tree business than just what the tree looks like. If it's the right one for us, it'll have a sticky-feeling trunk and when you run your hand along the branches the needles don't fall out. Or not very many anyway. Your dad can even bounce it on it's trunk to make absolutely sure it's not shedding needles."

"And it'll be taller than Daddy," Noah added confidently. Grabbing her hand to steady himself, he jumped over a wide rut in the path, totally unaware of the emotional havoc he caused Taylor by so easily putting his hand in hers, trusting her to keep him from falling. "He's really tall, you know. Just like a daddy's supposed to be."

Taylor found it hard to disagree as she looked ahead to the man searching among the trees farther down the row. Yes, indeed. Drew was everything a daddy was supposed to be—tall, involved, concerned, loving, dedicated. Unfortunately, he was also broad shouldered, intense, confident, and just plain desirable. All the things that made him dangerous for her.

As if he had radar, Drew turned his head toward her, his gaze stealing the oxygen from the air. A slow smile eased over his face as he noticed Noah's hand in hers. When he brought his gaze back to her face, it was full of approval. "I think I found what we're looking for."

She almost stumbled. He hadn't been looking at the tree. He'd been looking at her—with that same slow smile that signaled trouble. And she knew trouble when she saw it. Trouble was standing next to a Douglas fir, looking satisfied and sexy. She was beginning to hate it when he did that.

Pulling her along, Noah hurried to inspect the find, but he shook his head after only a few seconds.

"What's wrong with this one, buddy?"

"Taylor says the needles aren't supposed to fall off like that." He pointed to the carpet of needles beneath the fir.

"Okay. How about this one?" Drew pointed across the row to a Scotch pine.

"Not big enough," Taylor and Noah answered at the same time.

"Not big enough?" he echoed in dismay. As Noah walked ahead, Drew held Taylor back with a hand on her arm. "Wait a minute. What about all that practical advice you gave me? 'Buy a small tree because he won't know the difference. Noah's small, so any tree is going to look big to him. You won't have to buy as many ornaments.' Any of that ring a bell?"

"That was before."

"Before what?"

"Before I knew his personal yardstick for tall was his daddy. His tree has to be taller than you."

At the matter-of-fact pronouncement, Drew felt an undeniable catch in his breathing. Being a yardstick was a new experience, a wonderfully scary one. Every day, in moments like this, he was reminded of his responsibility to be there when his son needed him, to stand tall and frighten bogeymen that lurked in shadowy corners. More than anything he wanted to be there for his son.

"Okay," he said, clearing his throat. "Noah wants a monster tree. I can live with that, but answer this. You told me not to buy a bunch of ornaments this year, to wait and buy a few each year so they would mean something. So what are we going to use to decorate this towering tree that Noah has his heart set on?"

"Lots and lots of gingerbread men and cranberry garland."

"Oh." Drew let go of her arm and started after Noah. "Good plan."

"I thought so. Every year you add less gingerbread men and more ornaments."

After solemnly inspecting two-thirds of the trees on the lot, Noah made his selection, and Taylor completely agreed. According to the two of them, this was *the* tree. Hesitant to complain in the face of their enthusiasm, Drew looked at the tree and swallowed. He couldn't imagine anyone in their right mind wanting this particular tree. It was green, and it did smell like an evergreen. There, however, the resemblance ended.

The oddly proportioned blue spruce was over ten feet tall. The top of the tree sported two points, one slightly to the right of center. The crooked trunk and a broken branch contributed to the impression that this was a tree with a harsh history. His only hope now was that the tree would fail the "tests."

Drew grabbed hold of the trunk, near the middle, and gave it a good bounce, hoping for a shower of needles. No such luck. Taylor gave the tree one last inspection and decided the two really bare patches didn't matter because they could be turned toward the wall. Noah placed his hand on the trunk and pronounced it sticky enough. Praying for a miracle, Drew gave the tree one last shake—no needles fell off.

Catching the motion and the frown, Taylor almost felt sorry for Drew, and then she remembered he had asked for this. So she laughed and said, "Welcome to a Taylor Bishop Christmas. Now all we need is a few necessities."

By the time they got home, Drew had a whole new understanding of the term "necessities"—a tree stand, a tree skirt, tree lights, heavy-duty fishing line, glue, a box of soap flakes to mix up faux snow for the windows, cinnamon sticks, gold spray paint, glitter, a bag of big buttons, brown sugar, molasses, flour, an inch-wide paintbrush, extremely thin wire, and miles of holiday ribbon. Those were only a few of the items Taylor considered necessary.

When the Jeep rolled to a stop in their driveway, he and Noah looked at Taylor, "What now?"

"First we take all this inside and order pizza," she said.

"Pizza?"

"I haven't eaten since breakfast. The least you can do is feed me."

"And while we're waiting for pizza?"

"Noah and I unpack the Jeep." She held out her hand for the house keys. "Your job is to figure out how to put the tree in the stand."

"How hard can that be?" he asked.

Taylor got out and helped Noah down before she answered. "Technically, getting the tree in the stand isn't the problem. It's getting the tree to *stand* that's the trick. I must warn you," she said with mock severity. "Trees with character tend to resist conventional methods of display."

"A tree with character? Now there's a polite and kind description of our tree." Drew chuckled, then sobered. "You don't think I can do this!"

"Bingo. Come on, Noah, let's get this stuff inside before the snow flurries attack again."

Drew watched as she went round to the back of the Jeep and opened the tailgate. He slid out as Noah took a sack. Like a miniature work horse, his son trudged through the yard, his expression a study in concentration. When he set the sack on the porch, the little guy tramped back, head down, equally serious.

Sadly, Drew knew other children would have stopped to make snowballs out of the unmelted snow in the shade or tried to skate along the walkway in their rubber boots. Instead Noah was silently waiting for his next sack with his hands outstretched. Before he could decide how to cheer up his son, Taylor pretended to drop the sack she was giving him. Startled, Noah gasped and scrambled to catch it.

"Gotcha!" Taylor grinned and lifted the sack high.

When he realized she was playing, a tiny smile slipped out of whatever deep dark place his son hoarded them, and a soft giggle followed right behind it. The two of them were magic together, Drew decided as she handed over the sack. Taylor ruffled his hair, turned him around, and pushed him on his way, watching him with an expression that was heartbreakingly beautiful and terribly close to maternal.

In that moment Drew's longing for a real family and desire for Taylor got all tangled up again, just as they had all those years ago when he'd trailed in and out of the Bishop house. Separating one feeling from the other was impossible. And he had an idea that the more he was around her, the more impossible it would become.

Still smiling over Noah, Taylor grabbed the last two sacks from the back of the Jeep and gave the tailgate a hard shove with her hip. "Don't forget the tree stand. It's in the back seat. And don't forget to saw off about an inch of the trunk so the cut'll be fresh. Makes it easier for the tree to soak up water."

"I won't forget."

"Canadian bacon okay with you?" she asked, stopping beside him.

"My favorite."

In unison Taylor and Drew said, "Thin crust?"

Drew laughed. "That'll work."

"Good. I'll call," she promised as snow began fluttering down in fat flakes, one of them landing on the bow of her top lip.

Her pink tongue darted out to catch it, mesmerizing him, enticing him to explore her mouth. Without conscious thought, his hand cupped her face. When another flake fell, his thumb covered it the same instant it touched her bottom lip. The snowflake was a pinpoint of cold surrounded by the moist warmth of her mouth. Whether by accident or design, her tongue touched the pad of his thumb as he slid it across her lip.

The brief touch arced excitement through him, startling him with its intensity. How could something so fleeting, so simple, be so explicitly erotic? *Because it's subconscious foreplay.* That stroke of her tongue was an instinctive reaction to his touch. She knew it too. He could see it in her eyes, in the way she backed away, almost panicked.

"Well . . . I'd better get in. It's snowing. Noah's waiting. I have to call. Dinner." She turned and fled.

So many excuses. None of them honest. *You have to get away from me,* Drew corrected, as he pulled his pocketknife out and cut the hemp twine the Boy Scouts had used to tie down the tree. *Before you forget what it is that scares you so much.*

Taylor wasn't the only one tiptoeing across quicksand. He was in big trouble too. Doc Holiday wasn't the Christmas consultant any longer. She wasn't simply a friend lending a helping hand. She wasn't even just the woman he wanted to go to bed with. All of those things were normal, easily handled. None of those things worried him. What scared the hell out of him was wanting to wake up with her.

Life wasn't supposed to work this way. He was supposed to have time to get on his feet and learn how to be a dad before he found a woman who grabbed hold of his soul. And when he found that woman, she was supposed to hold on to him instead of figuring out ways to avoid him.

Taylor made herself comfortable on the off-white couch, stifled a giggle, and watched a familiar rite of passage—the one where the dad tells the son all about how to tie the Christmas tree to the wall with fishing line. Noah looked like a folded-up accordion with his knees and clasped hands hugged tightly to his chest as he squatted on the floor. The undecorated tree before him, which had crashed with suitable noise and fury only moments before, captured his complete attention.

After the crash Noah had patted the tree gently and told it not to worry. At that point Drew had leveled an irritated look at her and asked for the fishing line, which she just happened to have in her hand and offered without a hint of I-told-you-so in her voice. Then she had retired to the couch, stifling her amusement.

As she observed the two of them huddled together—brown head and blond—an unexpected contentment drifted over her, a comfortableness that was warmly seductive. There was a sweetness in watching Noah. At home she would have been refereeing fights and nagging Jason to wrap his presents in something more festive than newspaper. All of her boys were far too old and way too cool to worry about the bumps and bruises of a toppled evergreen or to look in her direction every so often to make sure she hadn't disappeared.

Careful, she warned herself. Don't romanticize this situation. This warm and fuzzy feeling is one of Mother Nature's little tricks of the trade to get everyone paired off and reproducing. Warm and fuzzy faded. She could testify to that. But it was wonderful while it lasted.

"Here goes," Drew said, and slowly removed his support from the tree.

He let his hand hover for a few seconds, waiting to grab the trunk if the tree started to lean again. It didn't.

Stepping back, he got his first good look at his handiwork. Tied to the wall, bare patches hidden, and in a shiny red stand, the spruce actually looked all right, better than all right.

"Told you so." Taylor got up from the couch and joined the two of them as they looked at the tree from the entrance hall archway. "With a few decorations and lights, it'll be a perfect tree."

"Perfect," Noah parroted, and spoiled the effect by yawning.

"But not tonight," his dad decreed. "It's bedtime, and we have to take Taylor home."

"You don't have to take me home!" For some reason she dreaded having him walk her to her door and say good night. "Mikey or Jason can come pick me up. I'll call home after Noah shows me his room."

"Why do you want to see my room?" Noah's question wasn't a complaint; it was five-year-old curiosity.

"Because I thought you might want to decorate it too."

"How we gonna do that?"

"I won't know until I see it, so I can tell your daddy what to do."

"Oh." He took her hand and pulled her toward the stairs. "This way."

"Okay. Drew, put water in the tree stand before we forget," Taylor ordered over her shoulder.

"Yes, ma'am. I'll even call your house. Then I'll be up to rescue you."

"Why will I need rescuing?" she asked.

"Because he never runs out of questions."

Taylor laughed and stepped up onto the landing. "I can handle questions, Hayseed."

"I'll come and rescue you all the same."

Noah's room turned out to be as bright and cheery and spotless as an ad in *Parents Magazine*. Unfortunately, Taylor subscribed to the theory that a clean room was the sign of a troubled mind. Her experience with small boys indicated that rooms were cleaned only after threat of bodily injury or if the boy in question was trying to make up for breaking a window. Drew didn't seem the type to threaten his son, and Noah didn't look like a kid who had ever broken anything.

"This is my room." He hiked his jeans up a notch. "I cleaned it up this morning. Roxie said, 'You can't be too careful this close to Santa Claus.'"

"She's right about that." How could she have forgotten the miracles Santa worked during December? Taylor hid her grin by making a show of turning round and round inspecting the room, mulling over the decorating possibilities. "I think we should put pretend snow on the windowpanes and wrap up your door like a package with a big, fancy bow."

"Can it be a shiny package, like silver or gold? I like silver and gold."

"Then silver and gold it is. If you wanted, we could put big Christmas bows on your stuffed animals too."

Noah shook his head.

"Oops, don't like that idea, huh?"

"I don't have any animals."

Startled, Taylor looked around the room again. She found books, balls, Lego blocks, action figures, and cars, but not a stuffed animal in sight, not even on the bed. "You don't have a bear or . . . or a bunny or something? Anything?"

Big, gray owl-eyes stared out at her from Noah's face. He shook his head. "Nope."

"That's okay," she assured him. "We'll think of something else to decorate." Taylor rubbed her hands together as if thinking of other wonderful treats. Mentally, she added another item to her shopping list; every child deserved a bear who gave unconditional love, who listened when no one else would, and who was never scared of the dark or the monsters in the closet.

Noah climbed up on his bed and untied his shoes as he spoke. "I know we got to keep you all day, and we had to stay up past bedtime, but since Christmas isn't fixed yet, do you think your mommy will let you come back real early tomorrow morning? I can get up real early if somebody wakes me up."

Such an innocent question, and one that sealed her fate with the same force as his shoes striking the hardwood floor. Would her mother let her come early? Her mother would insist. *Promise me, Taylor Marie. You won't forget what makes them happy. It's the little things. The things you'd least expect. Like saying yes sometimes when you should say no.*

Now was one of those times she should say no. Coming early and staying late put her in Drew's company. But she'd say yes. For Christmas anyway, she'd keep coming back as long as Noah wanted her, needed her.

Kneeling down in front of him and helping him off

with his socks, Taylor confided, "My mother died a long time ago, but I know for sure that she'd want me to come back early tomorrow. Maybe we can make snow angels if it snows a lot. Or better yet, we can make snow cream."

"How?"

"How what? How to make snow angels? Or how to make snow cream?"

"No. How do you know your mommy wants you to come back early?"

For a moment she was at a loss for words to explain how she knew. Finally she told him what was in her heart, knowing to a child it would make perfect sense. "Because the stars are shining, and she loved happy little boys more than anything in the world."

"Was she a good mommy?"

"The best."

"When she went away, did you want her to come back?"

"More than anything."

He thought about that for a few seconds, wiggling his toes and staring at them. Then in a low voice he wondered, "Is it okay if you don't want them to come back?"

"Them?" Taylor was afraid to ask, didn't want to know, but she had to be sure.

"Mothers who go away." His voice was so small, unsure as he repeated, "Is it okay if you don't want them to come back?"

Dear Lord, he's glad his mother is gone and he's ashamed, afraid that the feelings are bad or permanent. It was too heavy a burden for a child, and too complex a question to answer unprepared.

She cut her eyes at the door, praying for the cavalry to rescue her. Only a five-year-old could focus this completely on one issue and then steer every conversation toward the question they desperately wanted to have answered. In his mind they both had mothers who abandoned them. They were kindred spirits. The question he would never ask his dad was suddenly okay to ask her.

Feeling her way very carefully, Taylor answered, "I think it's okay to enjoy being with your dad and to want to stay here."

Noah looked her squarely in the eye and said, "Daddy is like your mommy."

"How is that?"

"He's the best."

Patting him on the knee, she said, "I think maybe you're right."

"About what?" Drew's voice entered the room a second before he did.

Taylor swiveled around in her kneeling position as Noah said, "We both think you're the best."

"Best *daddy*," Taylor clarified when Drew quirked an eyebrow at her. As she got up, she prudently changed the subject. "And both of us think we should get an early start tomorrow."

In fact, the more she thought about it, the better the idea seemed. Tomorrow was Monday; Drew would be at the bank, which meant she wouldn't have to worry about moments like the one by the Jeep. If she planned carefully, she could arrange to give Noah his Christmas and spend very little time in his dad's company.

"Can we?" Noah stood up on the bed, trying to be as tall as the grown-ups.

"Sounds like a good idea to me, buddy."

"Then it's settled," Taylor agreed, and smugly began to plan. "I've got a lot of shopping to do, so Noah can just go with me. I thought we'd go to the Enchanted Glade in the morning, and we'd bake the gingerbread men and decorate the house in the afternoon. You could come home at lunch and put the lights around the front door and the two potted shrubs."

Drew continued to nod his approval as she reeled off the schedule, not bothering to contradict her. Inwardly he doubted Taylor's day would run as smoothly as she planned. The first flaw in her strategy was the assumption that he'd be working tomorrow. He wouldn't. He wasn't scheduled to be in the office until January 2. But he wasn't going to say a word about that until tomorrow morning, when it was too late for her to change her plans.

Looking as if she'd just negotiated world peace, Taylor said, "Then all you'll have to do tomorrow night is decorate the tree."

"I believe I can handle that." A car horn honked outside. "Looks like Mikey's here. All right, buddy, you've got a big day tomorrow. Find your pj's while I walk Taylor to the door, and I'll be back to tuck you in."

Sliding off the bed, Noah said, "Night, Taylor. You

don't have to worry. Daddy'll make sure we get alarmed early."

"I'm sure he will. Night, Noah. See you in the morning."

Drew let her leave the room first and followed her down the stairs without saying a word. As they neared the door, she pushed up her sleeves, broadcasting her nervousness. They hadn't been alone for even a second since he'd wiped the snowflake from her lip. Silently he retrieved her coat from the banister and held it out.

She took the coat like a half-tamed cat, slowly reaching for the tidbit and then snatching it quickly. "Thanks."

"I'm the one who should be doing the thanking. I do appreciate you, Taylor."

"Really, it was nothing," she demurred as she put on the coat.

"I didn't say I appreciated what you've done, although I do. What I said was that I appreciate you. I appreciate the fact that you're warmhearted." He moved closer with every sentence. "I appreciate that you're bright. I appreciate that you're beautiful."

He was a millimeter away from kissing her when the car horn blared again, startling her. Taylor clutched her coat closed. "I . . . I have to go. Unless you have any more questions . . ."

Without missing a beat he opened the door. "You go on. I'll call you when I need you."

"Do that," Taylor agreed, and darted through the opening.

Only the tiny gasp he heard as he closed the door

assured him that she understood that he'd be calling her, but not about Christmas. Drew whistled all the way to the study. The phone book wasn't thick. Looking up the Bishop listings took only a second, and he found what he wanted. The Bishops had two phone lines.

SIX

A pink Princess phone sat in the exact center of the multicolored star-burst quilt that Taylor had added to the bed for warmth. She leaned against the headboard, propped up with pillows, staring at it. The tension was unbearable. She knew he'd call tonight. The only question was when.

During the entire drive home all she'd thought about was his suggestive promise to call her and how he'd tricked her into agreeing.

"I'll call you when I need you."

"Do that."

She had been so anxious to get to her room and turn down the ringer on the phone that she barely looked at Martha's decorating efforts, beyond noting that the outdoor tree lights were up, the candles were in the wrong windows, and Santa was on the roof instead of in the yard. Martha didn't seem to mind the absence of praise. Oh no, instead of pumping her for compliments, her sister-in-law busily pumped her for information about Drew. Faking a yawn had gotten her out of the conversation, but it also meant she had to stay in her room, where there was nothing to do besides stare at the phone.

When the call came, Taylor was still debating with herself about whether or not to answer. On the fifth ring, she swore softly, gripped the receiver, and lifted it to her ear. She'd just have to be blunt. That's all there was to it.

Taking a deep breath she said, "Drew, we have to talk."

"And hello to you too."

"Look, I know why you're calling. I appreciate the effort; I'm flattered. Really."

"Taylor—" he interrupted quietly.

"But I'm tired tonight," she explained. "I don't have the energy to carry on a regular conversation much less a sexy one."

"Taylor—"

"And to be absolutely honest, I'm not dressed for provocative. Now, if you want to discuss this freezer my dad calls a house, then I'm your girl. I've got on an oversized flannel nightshirt and white socks."

When she paused for a breath, Drew jumped in, his voice full of suppressed laughter instead of disappointment at having his erotic overture turned down. "Taylor, all I wanted was to know what time you'd be over tomorrow. We agreed on early, but we didn't discuss a time."

Taylor felt like four kinds of stupid. She put the

receiver to her chest and flopped back against the head-board, banging her head and forcing a sharp "Ouch!" at the contact. With her eyes closed and her index finger and thumb pressed to the bridge of her nose, she put the phone back to her ear.

"Taylor?" he inquired gently. "Taylor? Are you all right?"

"I'm fine." She let her hand fall to her lap. "Is eight o'clock okay?"

"Sounds perfect to me."

"Are you sure? It's not too late for you to get to work or anything? I could come earlier."

"No, no. Eight o'clock fits my plan perfectly."

"All right, I'll see you then."

"I'll be waiting." Drew's voice was whiskey-smooth and slid into her muscles and bones, heating her insides like a rum-spiced toddy. "Night, Taylor. You stay warm."

"Good night."

Very carefully she replaced the receiver. Much later she drifted off to a troubled sleep, alternately plagued by thoughts of Drew—the breathless, unsteady way he made her feel; and of Noah—the way the little guy held so much inside, how much she wanted to hear him laugh.

Morning and peace were a long time coming for Taylor.

Drew sat back on the couch and sipped a second cup of strong coffee as he waited for the doorbell to ring.

The fun was about to begin. He'd had a long time to think about last night's phone call. Taylor was going down for the count. He knew it and she knew it. What she didn't know was that Noah was going to deliver the knockout punch. Noah had plans for her, and so did his dad.

At exactly eight o'clock Taylor arrived.

"Daddy, she's here!" announced Noah, who'd been hovering in the entrance hall. When he opened the door, he waited for her to get inside and then said, "I'm ready."

After giving him a quick once-over, Taylor asked, "Don't you think you need some shoes, a coat, and maybe a hat?"

He lowered his voice to a theatrical whisper, "Do I have to wear my boots?"

"I was kind of hoping you would. It's still pretty slushy out there." She opened her black wool coat and pointed downward to where her blue jeans were tucked neatly into some knee-high mukluks. "I wore mine."

"Then I guess I gotta wear mine too." He didn't argue, but he sounded distinctly disappointed.

If he'd been like Mikey or Jason, she would have picked him up, turned him upside down, and shaken a giggle out of him. While she was shaking, she would have told him all the horrible things that happen to little boys without boots. However, intuition told her that Noah wasn't ready for such close physical contact. She had a feeling that he'd be scared of the roughhouse gesture instead of delighted. The thought made her sad.

Taylor put a hand on his shoulder. "Cheer up, Noah. Santa wears boots."

"His aren't red rubber."

"They were when he was little," she said in a tone of voice that implied *everyone* knew Santa wore red rubber boots as a child.

Perking up, Noah asked, "Cross your heart?"

"Cross my heart. Now, where's your dad?"

"The living room. I'll get my boots." He turned and padded up the stairs in his stocking feet.

When he disappeared, Taylor stuck her head in the living room and found Drew with his arm sprawled comfortably along the back of the couch by the fireplace. Uneasily she acknowledged her first impression upon seeing him. He was biding his time, waiting for something to happen or someone to arrive. He'd obviously been listening to the whole conversation.

Instead of a starched shirt and tie, he wore blue jeans and a great sweater patterned in midnight blue and cream. His boots were cowboy boots, and he rested one ankle on the top of the other knee. Startled by his casual appearance, Taylor asked, "Shouldn't you be getting ready for work?"

"I'm not scheduled to go into the bank until later," Drew told her, smiling smugly.

As he took another sip from the stoneware cup, she narrowed her eyes. If he got any more comfortable on that couch, he'd start putting down roots. Now she was really beginning to get worried.

"How much later?" she asked.

"January 2."

Once again, all her neat little plans came crashing down. Her hands clutched at the ends of her white muffler, strangling the soft cloth as if it were Drew's neck. In a depressed voice, she echoed, "January 2?"

"The vice president has been managing without Dad or me for a month now." Taking his time, Drew shifted his cup from one hand to the other by gripping it around the rim with his fingers. Then he transferred the cup to the coffee table and stood up. "I thought he could continue to manage without me for another couple of weeks until I got Noah settled in kindergarten here."

Slowly the significance of his words filtered through the denial clouding her brain. If he wasn't working, then he was free to go with them today! That was bad. Not a good idea at all.

Hoping against hope and not caring how rude she sounded, Taylor asked, "I guess you'll have the lights up by the time we get back?"

"Afraid not." He was enjoying this. He stood with his feet slightly braced apart and his thumbs hooked in the back pockets of his jeans.

"Oh? Are you going out?" she asked, praying that he had plans of his own.

"I kind of thought I might go out," he acknowledged, and looked pointedly at her.

"With us," she finished for him, resigned to the inevitable.

"That's right. With you and Noah. The three of us. Together."

The three of us. Taylor repeated the phrase in her

mind and hated it because it made her think of a family. A mommy and a daddy and Noah. The one scenario she wanted to avoid for the next few days because she was vulnerable.

Her emotions were too muddled, too entangled to separate real feelings from those created by her biological clock. Phrases like "the three of us" only confused her more. She wasn't getting any younger, and ever since she realized Noah looked more like her child than Drew's, the clock in her head had begun ticking more loudly than ever.

She could survive the Haywood men if she dealt with them separately, but she wasn't sure she could protect herself if they joined forces. Not anymore. Not after last night, after letting Noah inside her heart a little bit. Not after that kiss with Drew under the mistletoe.

"This Christmas means a lot to us," Drew whispered softly.

His voice was so close, she almost jumped. While she'd been lost in thought, he'd stolen up beside her, waiting and watching. He seemed never to tire of studying her. His brown eyes soaked up every detail, unnerving her and holding her all at the same time.

"Noah could hardly sleep last night," he told her. "He woke up in the middle of the night to ask me if I was 'no foolin'' sure the alarm clock was loud enough. And do you know what he said then?"

She shook her head, not because she didn't have a clue, but because she didn't want to know. Right now everything about Drew was too serious, too honest, too close.

"He said he wanted today to be the best, because if he was very good, he thought you might hug him. And he thought he might like that because you're such a nice lady. And you're soft. And you smell so good. And you even make him feel all warm inside sometimes."

Gently, he brushed a kiss against her lips. "I owe you one, Mouse."

Genuine gratitude was a hard thing to resist; it battered the walls that kept him out of her heart, kept him away from her real emotions. Noah had already breached those walls, creeping into her heart because he was a scared little boy who needed all the love his daddy could beg, borrow, or steal. And now Drew was creeping into her heart because he loved his son and wasn't ashamed to admit it. He had the courage to take on a job too many men would have refused.

For one insane moment, Taylor wondered how it would feel to be loved as completely as Drew was capable of loving. For a split second she wondered if Drew wanted her badly enough to beg, borrow, and steal her love. Next she simply wondered how badly he wanted her.

All she had to do was lean. All she had to do was flick her eyes down toward his mouth and he'd kiss her. Every instinct in her body understood the dynamics of this moment. One tiny motion and the pendulum would swing. Emotion would dissolve into desire; awareness would intensify to need. They were on the edge of intimacy, precariously balanced, motionless. Even breath was suspended as being too risky.

A second before she opened her mouth and lowered

her eyes, her self-protective instinct asked, *Is he worth giving up your freedom?* The question slammed through her, forcing her backward and away from temptation. The breath she'd been holding shuddered out of her in a horrified sigh at how easily he could make her forget the price she'd pay for falling into his arms.

Drew almost groaned in frustration, disappointment gnawing at him even as he tried to make sense of Taylor's actions. Coming so close to admitting she wanted him obviously scared the hell out of her. And backing away from that kiss was a reaction from so deep inside Taylor, he knew her fears weren't as simple as wanting to avoid long-distance relationships. He had only to look into Taylor's troubled blue eyes to see a reflection of the turmoil that reigned in her mind.

Dammit, he swore silently. He was back to square one in unraveling the mystery of why Taylor constantly put roadblocks between them. She wouldn't give up her secrets easily, so he'd have to be sneaky. As Noah joined them Drew smiled and began formulating questions to ask. Somehow he'd trip her up, make her speak before thinking.

Noah's eyes, as he looked at the entrance to the Enchanted Glade, were so wide, Drew thought they might swallow his face. Two firs towered beside the darkened entrance that was an arched opening near one end of a long wall. Shimmering faux snow weighed down the branches of each tree. A banner in Old English script hung above the entry, and more faux snow drifted artistically in piles beside the winding walkway leading into the exhibit.

"Was this always here?" Drew asked, casting around in his memory for a spark of recognition and finding none.

"No. They started this about five years ago. The people who owned the mall figured the Glade was an investment that would bring those holiday shoppers to the mall in droves. Just to make sure, they add something new to the display every year."

Assessing the line stretching out behind and in front of them, Drew had to agree about the exhibit's appeal. Morriston was roughly twice the size of Harvey, and it looked as though all sixteen thousand people, and then some, were here today. Slowly the line moved, and they advanced toward the entrance.

"What do you think about this, buddy?" he asked as he nudged him forward. His son nodded approval, but didn't say anything. Surprised at the low-key response, Drew started to ask the question again, but Taylor laid a hand on his arm.

"Trancelike states are common in five-year-olds faced with lumberjack hedgehogs." She pointed ahead. At the base of the fir tree on the left, a mechanical but realistic hedgehog tried to chop down the tree. "I wouldn't expect a whole lot of conversation out of him in the next half hour."

"There's more?"

"Just you wait," she promised him as they passed under the archway leading to the Enchanted Glade.

The dioramas inside were spectacular, from the polar bears who skimmed across the ice like professional figure skaters to the family of rabbits who opened presents beneath a Christmas tree decorated with bird nests, pine cones, and berries. Noah's pleasure was contagious. Even Taylor seemed to forget her vow to keep her distance from Drew, laying her hand on his arm, tugging at his sleeve, and sharing smiles with him every time Noah gasped with delight and said "ah."

As they stopped in front of the last scene, they saw Santa's tiniest reindeer trying to untangle himself from the sleigh harness as the elves shook their heads and loaded packages. Through the window of Santa's Workshop, they could see Mrs. Claus ironing Santa's red coat as he sat at his desk, pulling on his boots. For several minutes they watched the scene cycle through its program, always finding some new movement they had missed before.

When he heard a tactful cough from behind them, Drew put a hand on Noah's shoulder and an arm around Taylor's waist to steer them toward the exit. Having both of them in the circle of his arms felt right, felt like family was supposed to feel. Drew was silent as they left the mechanical animals, afraid that conversation would shatter the moment, and he wanted to hold on to it for as long as he could, until Taylor remembered she didn't want his arms around her.

Taylor felt Drew's touch and knew she should object, but couldn't. His subtle urging was the only reason she kept moving. Something had happened to her as she watched Noah's wonder and delight at each new treat. She stopped hearing the quiet hum of motors, stopped noticing the sometimes jerky movements of the remarkable creatures. She forgot what it was like to be an adult and remembered her childhood.

Inside the forest, she turned back time for a little while and touched the magic. Deep in her belly she'd gotten a flutter of excitement as they wove their way through the maze of scenes, each more elaborate than the one before. Anticipation replaced apathy. Suddenly she was looking forward to twinkling lights and off-key carols. And she had Noah to thank for it.

Glancing down, she saw him squint at the harshness of the mall lights as they moved out into the concourse after the dark of the Enchanted Glade. When she looked up, Leigh Madison, the most perfect woman in northern Arkansas, stood three feet away. Any hope she had of escaping unnoticed evaporated when Leigh did a double take.

"Drew? Drew Haywood? As I live and breathe, it is you! I heard you were back, but I live in Morriston now, so I haven't been by to see you."

Drew halted as she called his name and gave her a big smile as he guided them toward her. "Hello, Leigh! You look great. I'd like you to meet my son, Noah. You know Taylor, I believe."

Leigh's brows drew together as she obviously tried to put a name with the face. Calmly, Taylor endured the other woman's scrutiny, more conscious than ever of Drew's arm around her and what that wrongly implied about their relationship. Telling herself that the damage was already done, she stood her ground without pulling away from Drew.

When the connection finally clicked into place, Leigh said with some surprise, "You're Clay's younger sister, aren't you? You used to take piano from Momma when you were little."

"Yes, I am. I did."

"Well, darlin', you grew up gorgeous!" From another woman the remark might have been a snide commentary on Taylor's teenage appearance, but in Leigh's voice there was only admiration.

Perfect and charming, Taylor thought unhappily, remembering exactly why she'd never been able to warm up to Leigh. Well, the fact that she had dated Drew was partially responsible too. Leigh was an angelic vision of heaven on earth, all gold and white and . . . perfect. Around a woman like that, inferiority complexes flourished.

"Thank you," Taylor forced the simple response, cutting off the urge to demur, even though she felt positively grubby next to Leigh, who had on a ruffled blouse that defined "feminine"; who had a creamy leather coat, which was trimmed in fox, draped over her arm; and whose pale blond hair was swept up in a romantic profusion of curls.

Those curls spilled forward across her cheek as she inclined her head to study Noah. "Not only gorgeous, but I can see you've passed those good looks on to your son, Taylor."

"He's—" Taylor froze, clamping her mouth shut on the denial because a sixth sense warned her that the quick response might upset Noah, making him think she would be embarrassed to have him as a son.

A half second later Drew said, "Noah's my son. Since Taylor's home for Christmas too, she's giving us the holiday tour."

Without saying anything negative, his implication was clear—Taylor was not Noah's mother; subject closed. Mentally, Taylor gave him a great big hug for simply *claiming* Noah as his without mentioning his mother at all.

As if nothing unusual had happened, Leigh smoothed over the situation by saying to Noah, "Then you are one lucky boy. Taylor has a whole bunch of brothers. I bet she knows all the best places to take boys."

"You have brothers?" Noah asked as if the idea were the most exciting news he'd had all day.

"Six of them."

"Can they come over and play?"

Taylor laughed and combed his hair with her fingernails. " 'Fraid not, buddy. The youngest one is taller than me and too big for you. But you can come over to my house and play with my nieces and nephews."

"Okay." Noah waved his father close and whispered something neither of the women could hear.

Straightening, Drew cleared his throat and apologized, "Sorry, ladies, but it seems we need to make a pit stop. So if you'll excuse us?"

"You run right along, Drew," Leigh ordered. "I'll stay here and keep Taylor company. I'm waiting for my mother to finish up in the Hickory Farms store."

Taylor hoped she didn't look as deserted as she felt. Piped-in Christmas music played softly in the background, and Noah looked back once to check on her. She waved as they disappeared into the crowd. Turning to Leigh and grasping for a topic of conversation, she said, "How is your mother? Is she still teaching piano?"

"No, not anymore. She says her patience is failing in her old age."

Grinning, Taylor had to admit, "All those wrong notes, day after day, would try the patience of a saint."

"And believe me, she was no saint. I remember some awful knock-down-drag-outs during my teenage years. The only boyfriend we didn't fight about was Drew, and then there were the college years! Most of the time, I just wanted to trade her in on a new model." Leigh rolled her eyes. "You know how it is. How's your mo—"

Leigh cut off the word, but not quickly enough. A horrified expression consumed her face, and she put a hand to her throat. "Oh my God. I'm sorry, Taylor. It's been so many years. I didn't think. I would never— It was just one of those throwaway questions you ask people."

"It's okay," Taylor said aloud, but inside it wasn't all right. She would have given anything to have swapped embarrassing mother stories with Leigh, to have rolled her eyes and compared fights. But she couldn't. And nothing would ever change that fact. Christmas was all she had left of her mother—Christmas and the feelings Noah had helped her rediscover last night and today.

"I really am sorry," Leigh apologized again, regret evident in her posture and her tone.

"It's okay. Really." Somehow Taylor managed a reassuring manner. "You were right—it happened a long time ago."

Smiling oddly, Leigh shifted the coat to her other arm and said, "You know, we never did know each other very well. The only thing I really remember about you is that I used to get jealous because Drew had a soft spot for little Taylor Bishop. He was always leaving me to say hello to you, or looking your way because he didn't like the guys you were hanging out with."

Taylor gave a small huff of disbelief and shook her head. "You probably have me confused with Cissy Caldwell. She was a couple of years younger than you, but older than me."

"I don't think so, and if you need proof, all you have to do is take a good look at the man. He's still got a soft spot for you. He sure wasn't interested in taking his hand off your waist and giving this old girlfriend a hug. And by the way, he is one good-looking man."

Uncertain how to respond, Taylor simply gaped. She'd never *seriously* entertained the idea that Drew had been attracted to her too. There was that one kiss when she was sixteen, but that was it. Never another sign that he saw her as anything more than a cute kid.

"Now don't you worry, Taylor. I don't want him back. Not that I could get him," she added dryly. "Anyway, I'm already married to a wonderful man, and he gets cranky when I'm close to old flames."

Uncomfortable discussing what she and Drew were or weren't to each other with a virtual stranger, Taylor seized the opportunity to redirect the conversation to a safer topic. "How long have you been married?"

"Forever, it seems. I've got two kids and no time to call my own unless I sneak out of the house like today."

At that moment Leigh's mother walked up, delighted to see a former student. After a few pleasantries and Taylor's assurance that she still played now and again, they drifted away. No sooner had the crowd to her left swallowed them than the crowd on her right spit out Drew and Noah.

As they joined her Drew wiggled his eyebrows at Noah. "I bet they talked about us. Women always talk about you when you're not there to defend yourself."

Taylor felt her cheeks heat up with embarrassment. Drew noticed immediately. "So . . . what'd I miss?"

"Not much."

"Not much," he repeated, his tone doubtful.

A harried shopper bumped Taylor from behind, giving her the excuse she was looking for. Tearing her gaze from his suspicious one, she said, "Well, we'd better get our shopping done before this place gets busy!"

"Busy? This *isn't* busy?"

"It's six days before Christmas! Of course it's busy, but it's not lunchtime yet."

"I see your point. Onward, soldiers!"

Noah wanted to see Santa first, so they detoured. Drew and Taylor stood off to one side as Noah climbed solemnly up to the elevated platform and whispered with Santa, who chuckled and met Drew's eyes before giving a jovial, generic reassurance to the child on his knee, "All the good little boys are going to be happy this Christmas, so don't you worry. Santa's going to fix you up."

"Thank you," Noah responded politely and hopped off his knee. "Taylor said to ask you what kind of cookies you like."

"At your house I want chocolate chip!"

Relief shone on his face. "Oh good, she says that's her specialty."

Drew and Taylor were both fighting grins when Noah began to walk away, his mittens swinging from where they were clipped to the edge of his sleeves. Suddenly he stopped and turned back to Santa. "What color were your boots when you were little?"

Startled, Drew looked at Taylor, whose eyes were wide with apprehension. She shrugged her shoulders at him, conveying an unspoken question—*Who knew he'd actually ask Santa about the boots?* Drew was torn between fear that Santa would answer incorrectly, and laughter at Taylor as she edged into Santa's line of vision, pointing desperately at the red rubber boots on Noah's feet.

Either Santa was unusually astute or he saw her out of the corner of his eye. "Red. They were red. I always loved those boots. They don't make 'em for grown-ups, so I have to wear black now."

Standing a little straighter, Noah walked off the platform as Taylor mouthed a "thank you" to Santa. Laughing, Drew scooped up his son and reached for her hand. "I don't know how you do it, Mouse, but this was exactly what I had in mind when I asked for a Taylor Bishop Christmas."

The rest of the morning was just as satisfying to him. More often than not, Noah walked between them, holding on to each of their hands and offering his opinion on the ornaments they collected. They found a mouse wearing a muffler and red boots; crystal icicles to dangle from the branches; and a Star of Bethlehem to put on top.

But the pièce de résistance was an inexpensive wooden ornament that Taylor unearthed from the bottom of a barrel marked two dollars. Holding up the decoration, she declared this was the first in the collection Noah would take with him when he married. In her hand she held an ark complete with giraffe heads poking out the windows.

"We can go home now," she announced.

Drew didn't argue. The lady knew exactly what she was doing.

By midafternoon a garland of greenery, tied with festive red bows, undulated gracefully along Drew's staircase. The outdoor lights were strung, and the smell of just-baked gingerbread men permeated the house. Drew paused at the kitchen door and enjoyed the sight of Noah double-checking his men to make sure they all had eyes. The counter was littered with boxes of confectioner's sugar and food coloring; molasses and butter wrappers; and tins of allspice, cinnamon, and nutmeg. Noah had a bath towel pinned around his neck to protect his clothing, and Taylor had a dish towel wrapped around the front of her jeans and tucked in the sides.

Finishing his inspection, Noah discovered a missing eye. He took care of it instantly. "Okay, Taylor. They can all see. What do I do now?"

Glancing over at the kitchen table, she said, "Very good! Why don't you give them some bow ties while I put some red coloring in the icing for the smiles?"

"Can I make them buttons?"

"Absolutely. Give 'em buttons, bow ties, and anything else you want."

Noah went back to work on his masterpieces, and Taylor returned to her icing. As Drew walked softly toward her, she stole a taste of icing with an index finger and glanced at Noah to be sure he hadn't caught her. A second before the finger disappeared into her mouth, Drew grabbed her wrist and held it, pulling her around to face him.

"Can I have a taste?"

"Sure, Daddy," Noah volunteered without looking away from his decorating. "Just leave enough for the smiles."

"I'll only take this little bit," Drew promised as he brought Taylor's finger closer to his mouth.

SEVEN

Taylor tried to tug her hand free, but the first effort was weak, delayed by surprise, and then it was too late. Every muscle in her body tensed as his tongue bathed the pad of her finger, urging it into his mouth. Already the first pulse of desire was rippling through her. She shut her eyes. She couldn't watch. She certainly didn't need to look at him as he closed his sensual mouth over her finger. Her sense of touch was devastating enough without adding sight.

The wet heat of his tongue cradled her finger, pushing and pulling along the tip, savoring the sugary glaze that coated her skin. When he began to suck in earnest, her breath caught in her chest. Over and over, she kept telling herself that her heart should not be pounding, that he was only sampling the icing. Over and over again her body's response called her a liar.

Her blood was hot. The moment was hot. No matter how innocent, this was sex, pure and simple. This was heat responding to heat. This was how she wanted to feel in the dark with no clothes on and plenty of time. The coward in her hated feeling this way.

Why does it have to be you?

Drew gave her finger one last brush of his tongue and then softly said, "What do you mean—why does it have to be me?"

Her eyelids snapped up, and she snatched her hand from his grasp before he could capture it again. "Wh-what?"

"You said something."

"No I didn't," she insisted quickly, horrified at the possibility.

"Yes you did," Noah piped in. "You said—"

"That's okay, buddy," Drew interrupted, secretly pleased with his son's perfect timing. "She remembers now. Don't you, Taylor?"

"I was just talking to myself. It was nothing important," Taylor assured him. Then she ignored him by busily putting the red icing in a wax paper cylinder and nicking the tip with scissors so Noah could squeeze out smiles onto the faces of all of his men. "Ready for the red, Noah?"

"Yes, ma'am. They all have buttons now." He handed her the old icing tube and wiped his hands on the striped bath towel that covered him. When he took the red icing, he was careful not to squeeze the tube on his way to the table where the gingerbread men were spread out like little toy soldiers in battle formation.

"Need some help there, buddy?" Drew asked.

"Taylor says I'm big enough to do the job. She trusts me."

"In that case, Taylor and I are going to go in the living room and straighten out a few things."

"I've got to clean up this mess I made," she argued. "I never was a neat cook."

Drew grabbed the dish towel tucked around Taylor's waist as she hung back. The towel came off, and he tossed it into the sink, covering up the bowls, spoons, beaters, and measuring cups. "All cleaned up."

"You need to put the lights on the tree," Taylor warned him as he reached for her arm. "The gingerbread men are going to be ready in a little while. We'll have to decorate the tree."

He pulled her along with him. When they were out of easy earshot of Noah, he promised, "I'll light the tree right after I light a fire."

"You don't have any firewood," she pointed out.

"It's not that kind of fire." Drew pulled her up hard against him, settling his hands around her waist and then sliding them to the small of her back.

The kiss was sealed not with his lips but with his body. Hard planes met soft curves. Faith confronted doubt. Want satisfied need, and sparks flew as his mouth finally came down on hers.

He held nothing back as his hands slid along her hips and his fingers found the sweet rounded contour of her rump to lift her up, against his arousal. Sugar and cinnamon made her taste sweet and hot, like heaven and hell. Her surrender was slow but complete. Her hands crept up his arms and around his neck until her breasts were pressed full against him.

When Drew pulled his mouth from hers and began a sensual descent to the hollow at the base of her throat, Taylor instinctively arched her neck to give him access. She caught her breath as his tongue teased the hollow and his palm skimmed up her rib cage to flirt with the underside of her breast, which suddenly felt full and heavy and needy. Deep in the juncture of her thighs she felt a pulse flicker, a tiny throb that stole her breath.

She wasn't innocent, but she'd never felt like this in a man's arms, never felt completely overwhelmed by the possibility of intimacy. Emotion buckled her knees, but instinct kept her on her feet, telling her this was right, urging her to push her hips forward, rub herself against him, and silently ask him to ease the ache within her. She shifted her weight, slid upward and down. The contact sent a shiver through her and dragged a soft moan from her throat.

At the unexpected sound she froze. Common sense finally loosened the stranglehold desire had on her and dashed cold water along her nerve endings. She couldn't let her body make a decision for her heart. Twisting away, she glanced first at the kitchen door and then back at Drew. As she pushed up her sleeves, she asked in a pitched whisper, "Have you lost your mind?"

"No, just my patience," he snapped, reaching for her again, cursing softly when she sidestepped him. "How long are we going to play this game, Taylor?"

"I don't know. How many times do I have to say that nothing is going to happen between us?"

"I don't know," Drew shot back angrily. "Which one of us are you trying to convince?"

In that moment Taylor faced the inescapable truth. Convincing him wasn't the real problem; convincing her hormones was. He was right, but she would have bitten a hole in her lip before agreeing with him. She made a show of looking toward the kitchen again, implying that Noah might overhear the conversation.

"He couldn't care less about us right now," Drew told her flatly. "You're going to have to deal with what's between you and me."

"There is no you and me!"

Drew crossed his arms and lowered his voice. "There's no Santa Claus either, but that doesn't stop us from creating him for Noah. Reality is what you make it, Taylor. There could be a you and me if you were willing to work with me on it!"

"Now, isn't that just like a banker? Thinking you can balance everything in life by taking something from column A and putting it in column B and then adding it all up again! You think you can fix anything with a little adjustment, a little compromise. Well, it doesn't work like that in the real world, because sometimes compromise simply isn't enough. People aren't numbers you can add and subtract until you get what you want."

"Going after what I want doesn't make me the bad guy. Going after you doesn't make me the bad guy. In the real world everybody wants something. *Everybody*." Drew put his hands on his hips. "Even you want something."

"Nothing I can have." The truthful response slipped

out before she could censor it, leaving her vulnerable, stripped bare in a way she had never been before.

After a long pause, he said, "No more guessing games, Taylor. Just tell me. What do you want?"

It wasn't an order, but she felt compelled nonetheless, compelled to make him understand that some problems were too basic to solve. Compromise wasn't always enough. Sometimes sacrificing one dream for another was the only solution. Like now—she wanted a carefree life of her own, and she wanted Drew. She could have one or the other, but not both.

"Tell you what I want?" she echoed softly. "Let's start with the fact that I'm twenty-nine years old and I want my mother back. Sometimes I want her to tuck me in and tell me everything is going to be okay. Can you fix that, Drew?"

Stunned, Drew met her steady gaze, knowing that she'd just admitted something intensely private, something she'd never told anyone else, and he felt every bit as helpless as she'd wanted him to feel. Score one for the lady, he decided as she stared him down.

"You know I can't fix it," he said.

"Yeah, well, get used to it. Everything I want is that tough. It always has been. All my choices are black or white."

"They don't all have to be that way."

She laughed humorlessly. "Oh, but they are. Reality isn't what *we* make it. Reality is reality, and I learned a long time ago that you have to deal with it. Even if you don't want to."

Drew started to argue, wanting to know what any of

this had to do with their relationship, but a terrified wail from Noah grabbed his attention. There was heartbreak in his son's cry, gut-wrenching emotion that stopped the blood in his veins. Taylor moved a split second faster than he did, racing toward the kitchen. When they got there, Noah looked at Taylor and began to cry harder, circling away from her and behind the table. His face was flooded with color, and his gray eyes reflected regret and trouble. Tear tracks testified that he'd probably been crying for a while.

"What's wrong, Noah?" Taylor asked.

In between sobs, he forced out, "I only . . . w-wanted them to . . . s-sing. I didn't . . . m-mean to r-ruin them."

In unison, both adults looked down at the gingerbread men, who had big sloppy *O*'s instead of smiles. Some of the *O*'s were so big, the top of the loop crossed through the eyes. Some of them were more like triangles than circles. Some of them looked as though he'd tried to scrape off blobs of icing where the circle connected messily.

"They aren't ruined," Taylor said as calmly as she could manage, considering the constant stream of ragged "I'm sorry's" coming from Noah, who unconsciously kneaded the terry cloth towel with his hands.

As frustration welled up from the pit of her stomach, her mind raced. She couldn't care less about the gingerbread men, but she realized she cared a great deal for the little boy cowering on the other side of the table. Seeing Noah gripped by such disappointment and fear was almost more than she could stand. Her heart raced too, pounding a pulse in her throat. All she could think about was Drew's confession to her that Noah wanted everything to be perfect.

Why? The possible answers to that question terrified her.

Stealing a look at Drew, she could tell that he was still in shock and probably hadn't reasoned far enough ahead to worry about why this was happening. Shock was probably good for him right now, she decided. He hurt for Noah. That much was obvious in the look of pain on his face. She wasn't sure he could handle anything else. He was still so new at being a parent.

After several tense moments Noah wiped his sticky hands across his eyes and shook his head. "They're r-ruined. You trusted me, and I r-ruined Christmas."

This time the significance of the word "ruined" hit her, and her jaw clenched. Such a grown-up concept for a child. He didn't say "broken" or "messed up." He said "ruined." Not said—*repeated* the word was more like it. He repeated a word that had obviously been used on him again and again, enough times for him to get the pronunciation right.

Making a gesture at the table, she told him, "A real Christmas can't be *ruined* by cookies. I think you did a wonderful job. I never had a choir of gingerbread men."

A shuddering sigh went through Noah as a tear trailed down his face and he confessed what he thought was the biggest crime of all—his disobedience. "I was supposed to make smiles."

"She said to make anything you wanted," Drew said softly, finally finding his voice. Watching his child come apart had scared the hell out of him, torn his heart out. He'd never seen Noah like this, completely terrified, out of control, making himself sick with emotion over something so insignificant as gingerbread.

"Daddy!" Noah said, as if just realizing he'd disappointed his father too.

"It's okay, buddy." Drew took a step toward him.

"No!" Noah backed up. "It's not okay. I m-messed up everything. Santa said only the good little boys get what they want! I tried, but I messed it up for us, Daddy. I haven't been good at all." The words tumbled out of him rapid fire. "I r-ruined Taylor's cookies."

"They're your cookies," Taylor interrupted firmly, instinctively realizing that Noah needed logic as much as reassurance. "Nobody's going to be mad at you for making cookies with character."

At that his gaze swung back to her. "Like the Christmas tree?"

"Exactly like the Christmas tree," she agreed, projecting as much acceptance and pleasure as she could.

Noah looked at her hopefully for a second, then frowned. His lip quivered, but he was definitely calmer than before. "They were for our tree. For decorations."

"They're still for our tree," Drew assured him, and walked around the edge of the table, feeling as though he'd won a small victory when Noah didn't back up again. "We'll have the only gingerbread choir in town."

"I disobeyed Taylor." He was watching his father's reaction carefully.

"No you didn't, buddy. You used your imagination."

"I don't like wearing my boots," Noah said, determined to make a clean breast of everything. "And I get mad about it when you're not around."

Drew chuckled and swooped him up. He remembered how Taylor cajoled the boys out of bad moments by teasing them with outrageous comments that put their absurd fears in perspective.

As he started to flip Noah upside down Taylor realized his intention. She got out a raspy "No!" But it was too late; Drew wasn't listening.

Panic seized her, rooting her in place and freezing time. She was unable to look away, petrified of the scene to come. Drew was about to make a horrible mistake, and she couldn't stop him. He didn't realize that her brothers and Noah were as different as night and day. This wasn't a normal five-year-old fit or a ploy for attention. Noah's very real fears were still lurking too close to the surface. They were still too sharp.

"Okay, Mr. Wise Guy," Drew teased with a chuckle, "you've convinced me. You're just too much trouble for an old man like me. I guess I'll have to trade you in on a new kid."

"No! I don't have anywhere else to go!"

The soul-piercing screech cut though Drew like hot steel and unnerved him. Instantly he pulled Noah back up into his arms. He floundered for words as great tearless sobs wracked his son's tiny body again. A glance at Taylor for support only confirmed his worst fear. He saw the knowing look in her eyes and felt as devastated as his son must be. A good father would never have done this.

How could he have terrified his own son like this? How

could he not have known? He'd made a mistake that should never have been made, and now all he could do was whisper apologies that Noah wouldn't hear and try to hug a child that refused to be comforted. "I'm sorry, Noah! I'm sorry, buddy. I would never trade you. I love you more than anything, son. Don't you know that by now?"

Little hands and arms pushed hard against his chest, and his son screamed for Taylor, looking her way, desperately begging, "Taylor, please will you take me? I wanna go with you. *Please.*" He was all twisted around in Drew's arms as he pleaded, "You love the trees that aren't perfect. You won't send me away when I'm bad. Can't you love me too? You don't have any little boys of your own. *Please.*"

The last word broke on a sob, and also broke her heart. But that was nothing compared to the way the sob crushed Drew. Anguish transformed his face, dulling his eyes with misery. She could see the muscles of his jaw tighten as he fought the tears that threatened. Noah's small pitiful plea had ripped his heart out, and there was nothing she could do to stop the bleeding.

"*Taylor!*" Noah was holding his arms out to her now, kicking to be free of his father.

Defeated, Drew let him slide to the floor, watched his son fling himself into Taylor's arms, watched her cradle and soothe him. For the second time that night he felt absolutely helpless. In a couple of days she had learned more about how to love Noah than he had in two months. When he couldn't stand to watch anymore, he walked away. He was useless. However unintentionally, he'd hurt the one good thing in his life.

Drained emotionally, he halted in front of the fireplace, resting his forearm on the mantel, a hand on his hip, and closed his eyes against the pain of failing. From the kitchen he could hear Taylor murmuring nonsense in a voice that was strong and gentle, full of love. He heard her as she crossed the room behind him, still softly reassuring Noah, but he didn't turn around. He knew he wasn't needed. Taylor had everything under control, as always. Then he heard her climb the stairs, heading for Noah's room.

Self-loathing ate at his soul as relentlessly as an animal caught in a steel trap gnaws at its own leg, oblivious to the pain. Drew snatched a pinecone off the mantel and flung it as hard as he could across the room. The cone exploded against the wall, flaking off a chip of paint and leaving traces of glitter. With a disgusted shake of his head Drew remembered too late that it was Noah who had painstakingly shaken glitter onto the outer edges of the cones after Taylor had swiped them with glue. And now he'd destroyed one of them.

The silence of the house crowded in on him, rebuking him. Finally he walked over to pick up the broken decoration and held it in his hand, wondering why it was so easy to destroy and so difficult to create. But that wasn't really true. At least not for Taylor. She knew how to love; she never hurt anyone. She didn't have a destructive impulse in her body.

He looked upward, in the direction of his son's

room. She was up there now, trying to pick up the pieces of his son's shattered trust. No wonder she was afraid of him, of intimacy in their relationship. He'd destroyed a five-year-old's trust with a thoughtless, stupid remark. God only knew what he'd do to her, given the chance. He'd never been really good at loving anyone.

Drew's hand closed around the pinecone, squeezing hard enough for the remaining sharp spines to cut into his hand, but he didn't notice.

Taylor scanned Noah's room, looking for a warm, soft place to curl up and ride out the storm, only to be disappointed. There was no rocking chair, no easy chair, no soft, safe corner in which to cuddle, and she didn't dare suggest any of those additions to Drew. That would be one more bit of guilt he'd heap on himself, regardless of the fact that he couldn't be expected to think of everything.

He seemed to have picked up some foolish idea that good parents didn't make mistakes. Well, she'd disabuse him of that notion the minute she got back downstairs. The real truth was that good parents never made the same mistake twice. Or at least not very often.

Sniffing loudly, Noah readjusted his grip on her neck, which was a blessing since her neck was beginning to ache. As Taylor sat down on the bed, rocking back and forth, she realized the shoulder of her blouse was actually wet from his tears. There was probably a little runny nose thrown in for good measure. She almost smiled at the memories the damp sensation recalled.

Instead of pushing him away, she held him tighter. Her shoulders had been wet before, and ridiculous as it sounded, she'd missed it. Not the soggy shirts, but the other part—cuddling a warm little body next to hers and feeling a child's trust seep into her bones, making her feel special. Noah had formed an attachment to her, and she to him. She hoped it was as simple as the fact that they'd both lost a mother.

Time passed. She rocked, and she waited, not wanting to rush Noah. Right now both he and his father needed time and a safe place to let go of their hurts. The two of them were the emotional equivalent of the walking wounded. All she could do was hug the smallest one and hope the other one wouldn't punish himself too badly before she could get downstairs and repair the damage to his dream of being the perfect parent.

Shaking her head, she recognized that she sounded like a regular Florence Nightingale—no, she sounded like a regular Doc Holiday; the quintessential strong Southern woman, holding the family together in time of crisis. Everything she'd promised herself that she'd never have to be again.

Then why didn't you hand Noah to his father and run like hell?

Because no one with a scrap of human decency would have run, she argued.

Liar. Noah is Drew's problem, not yours.

As she debated with herself she continued to rock the child in her arms, finding comfort in her actions.

Why hadn't she walked away? What was it about her that couldn't say no to these two?

Glancing down at the blond head, she admitted that Noah got to her. Just like his dad. In a few short days they'd managed to sneak past her defenses. She cared about them. Not enough to give up the rest of her life, she assured herself quickly, but enough to want their happiness.

"You okay now, buddy?" she ventured finally.

His answer was another sniff and a halfhearted nod.

"Good. Can you sit up and talk to me for a little while?"

His arms slipped away from her neck, and he said, "Yes, ma'am."

Sometimes polite children were downright scary, Taylor thought. Her boys would have said, "Yeah" or "If I have to." But not Noah. Even in crisis he remembered his manners, and it made him seem so fragile. She started to shift him off her lap, but he tensed up, ready to clutch her again. So she settled him back down on her thighs. Five was such a difficult age—not quite a toddler, not quite a big kid.

"I think I need to tell you about my little brothers," Taylor began, and went on to tell him about her family, about how she and her mother had always turned her brothers upside down, tickling and teasing them when they were being silly or unhappy about something. "And the boys always knew that we never meant anything we said when they were upside down. That was part of the game, and they used to pretend to be sad so I would pick them up. Your daddy was only playing the game we played at my house."

"He said he was too old to have a bad little boy," he whispered to his kneecaps.

"But he didn't mean it. You were upside down," Taylor reminded him. She burrowed her fingers under his chin, which seemed glued to his chest, and lifted his face. His hair stuck up at an odd angle from where he'd pressed against her, but she resisted the urge to fix it. Capturing his gaze, she continued, "And now he's sorry he ever said it. He loves you a whole bunch. I can tell about these things."

He worried his bottom lip with his teeth. "Mommy said if I was bad, he'd give me away."

Outrage did not begin to describe her reaction. Her smile slipped for a moment before she could recover enough to stammer, "She must have been kidding or . . . or something. Why would you believe that?"

"Because that's what grown-ups do."

"No. No, it isn't, Noah. People who love you don't just give you away."

"That's what Mommy did. And I told her I was sorry." Gray eyes bored into hers, urging her to believe him. "I didn't mean to."

A chill stole its way up her spine, but she refused to shiver. She couldn't let Noah think anything he said would frighten her or change how she felt about him. She hated to think of him living with all of this bottled up inside. For whatever reason, he'd chosen her as his confidante, and she couldn't let him down.

Calmly she combed his hair into a semblance of order with her fingertips, and asked, "Didn't mean to do what?"

"To argue about the boots."

Her hand stilled. "The boots?"

"I hate wearing boots. They make my feet hot." Noah avoided her gaze, fiddling instead with the gold filigree locket she wore around her neck. "I didn't mean to argue, but I forgot. She warned me, but I forgot."

"Warned you?"

He nodded and then looked up. Tears pooled in the corners of his eyes. "She told me if I was bad one more time, she was going to give me back to Daddy. But I forgot, and I wouldn't wear the boots, and she left me with Daddy. And now Daddy doesn't want me either."

Appalled, Taylor realized he had it all worked out in his mind. That's why he was so quiet, so determined to do everything right. In his mind being perfect equaled being loved. To Noah, the evidence fit together so neatly, so reasonably, when in reality his mother's leaving him was so much more complicated than a scene over those damned red boots. His experience was the only one from which he could draw conclusions, and those conclusions were wrong.

She did shift him off her lap then, angling toward him and holding on to his shoulders so he would know how deadly serious she was. "Honey, I don't know your mother"—*And I hope I never meet her*, she added silently —"but I know your daddy. I've known him a long time. When I was younger, I thought he was the strongest, kindest man I'd ever met. I still think that. He doesn't care about boots or gingerbread men. He cares about you. He loves you, and he's never, ever going to give you away or trade you in on a new kid."

"How do you know that for sure?" The tears receded, and Noah's voice was stronger, daring her to convince him. He wanted to be convinced, and she counted that as a good sign.

"Because he told me so before I ever met you. And your daddy doesn't lie. He was very proud of you." Rubbing his hands with hers, Taylor said, "He still is."

Noah shook his head quickly, his emotions obviously still on the roller coaster. "Not now. I wasn't very nice. I screamed and kicked him."

"Then maybe you should say you're sorry."

He looked down, nervously pulling on one index finger, afraid to hope and desperately wanting to believe the solution could be so simple. "Will that make it okay?"

"No. I think you'd probably need to give him a hug too."

In a very small voice, Noah said, "I can do that. I'm a very good hugger. Daddy taught me. Wanna see?"

"Yeah, I think I do."

Noah got up on his knees and wrapped his arms around her, squeezing and making "umm-umm" sounds. Taylor squeezed back and let Noah decide when to stop. After a few seconds he dropped back onto his heels and said, "See?"

"That is definitely the best hug I have ever had."

"No, Daddy does the best hugs. You need to get him to hug you. When he's not mad at me anymore, I could ask him to hug you if you want."

Out of the mouths of babes, Taylor thought. "That's okay, buddy. I'll ask him myself." *Not!* She smiled.

"Okay." He struggled to untangle a shoe from folds in the bedspread and to get his legs out in front of him so he could slide down. "Come on. Daddy says men are supposed to make a 'pology real quick when they get something wrong or hurt somebody's feelings. If they don't, they're jerks. I don't want Daddy to think I'm a jerk."

"You could *never* be a jerk," Taylor said.

When he grabbed her hand and dragged her down-stairs, all Taylor could think was how amazing children were, how easily they could travel the emotional dis-tance between despair and poise. Probably because they didn't have as much pride mixed up in their emotions as adults did. She tipped her hat to Drew for teaching Noah that making a sincere apology was always a prior-ity. If you could teach a child to think, to be kind, and to be responsible, everything else worked itself out.

She almost stumbled on the stairs as she realized that this was advice she should take to heart. It was time to stop worrying about Mikey—Mike—no one called him Mikey anymore except her. It was time to let go and let him make his own choices about life and college. Her job was over, and that scared her to death.

What was it her mom always said? *One door closes, and another one opens.* Well, that didn't mean she had to step through, she told herself just as Noah readjusted his grip on her hand, pulled her into the living room, and into the middle of a family. For a second she thought about slipping away, but then Drew's eyes found hers, and she was trapped.

Daddies weren't supposed to be sexy or vulnerable. But Drew was both, and he needed her. Whatever happened next, she was a part of it.

EIGHT

When Taylor and Noah appeared in the doorway, Drew felt the world grind to a halt, as if nothing else could be decided or enjoyed until he'd made peace with his son. Waiting had been a purgatory of sorts—tense and lonely and full of hindsight. Three or four times he'd gotten as far as the stairs before making himself return to the living room. Each time, he'd had to remind himself that his son trusted Taylor. And so did he.

It was hard not to trust her. She had a way with people that made them want to get closer. No, it was more than that. She was an emotional magnet for lost souls; she knew what people needed and gave it. Even before helping the homeless became fashionable, she'd turned the high school Christmas float into a toy factory for underprivileged kids. Every year, the float was loaded with toys donated by the crowd en route.

As he watched her standing beside his son, Drew realized she always gave much more than she got. Like this Christmas. Like patching up his mistake with Noah. Maybe that was the secret to loving someone—to give more than you took.

The second Noah let go of her hand, Drew dropped to his knees and held out his arms. Rushing into them, Noah buried his face against his dad's chest. Drew rocked from the impact, but steadied himself.

Lord, it felt good, holding his son, knowing he hadn't destroyed the bond he'd been working to build since he got him back. He raised his head and mouthed a heartfelt "thank you" to Taylor. She shrugged as if it were nothing, but he knew better. To him it was everything, and he wouldn't forget.

After squeezing his son tight, Drew managed to get out his carefully rehearsed speech—the one he'd written and rewritten in his head during the last forty-five minutes. "I didn't mean what I said about trading you in, Noah. I want you here, with me. You're my son, and I'm going to hold on to you for a long, long time because I love you, and nothing is ever going to change that. *Ever.*"

"Promise?"

"Cross my heart," Drew said. When Noah hugged him again, Drew glanced over at Taylor, who nodded her approval, which meant almost as much to him as his son's understanding.

"I didn't know it was a game, Daddy," Noah told him, looking up and claiming his attention again.

"Well, it wasn't a very good game, and we won't be playing it again, buddy."

"Oh, but I know what it means now. It's okay. Taylor says I'm not supposed to believe you when I'm up-side down. Those are all the things I'm not supposed to worry about because you're bigger and stronger and won't let them happen. It's sort of like you're saying 'I love you' but backwards." He turned his head. "Isn't it, Taylor?"

She nodded. "Absolutely."

"See?" Noah said to his dad. In a very patient voice he asked, "Got it now?"

"Got it." The last bit of the blackness chewing on the edge of his soul receded as Drew repeated, " 'I love you' but backwards."

"Yes, sir. Oh—I forgot." Suddenly remembering his important apology, Noah stood up straighter. "I don't wanna be a jerk. I'm sorry I yelled, and I won't kick anymore."

"And I'm sorry I scared you. I'll try never to do that again." He enfolded Noah in his arms for another quick hug, hungry for tangible proof that his son still trusted him.

"Daddy?"

Leaning away from him, Drew looked down. "What?"

Noah motioned him closer and cupped a hand around his ear as he confided, "Taylor hugged me, and she's soft, and she smells like flowers. Can she spend the night with us?"

Choking on laughter and then coughing to clear his throat, Drew looked up at Taylor, whose brow was fur-rowed from the effort of trying to hear. Caught eaves-dropping, she looked away quickly. He grinned and wished he could share the joke with her, but something told him she wouldn't find it nearly as funny as he did. With genuine regret, he said, "No, buddy, I don't think so."

"Then can she stay for dinner?" Noah asked, forgetting to whisper.

"Now, *that* I can ask her. Will you stay?" He tried to keep his tone casual, tried not to insinuate any other invitation, but his eyes betrayed him, asking for more. It was becoming increasingly difficult to look at her and not want more. "Will you have dinner with us?"

Taylor hadn't counted on staying so late. When she had arrived that morning, her plan had been to have the house finished, the tree decorated, and herself out of there by dinnertime, but the gingerbread crisis had put a very large crimp in her plans, upsetting the whole schedule. Deep inside she knew that being in a house with Drew at night was only asking for trouble.

When she didn't answer right away, Noah swiveled in his father's arms to add his encouragement. "Please. I'll cook cereal."

"How could I resist such a charming offer?" she replied finally, throwing her hands wide in defeat. Inwardly she salvaged her pride by telling herself that she had to talk to Drew about Noah. Wanting to stay had nothing to do with her answer. She *had* to stay. To talk about Noah.

"I think we can do better than cereal," Drew insisted. "How about grilled cheese and soup?"

"I like grill cheese," Noah volunteered.

"I know that!" Drew tousled his son's hair and

scooped him up. He looked like a man with a new lease on life. "I was asking Taylor."

"They're two of my favorites."

She didn't take her eyes off him as he stood up with Noah still in his arms, realizing that she could just as easily have been talking about the two of them. They were special together. They had a kind of magic between them that held her spellbound in a way her own family never had. She had never got all misty-eyed when her dad had picked up the boys. She had never got this unexplained sense that all was right with the world.

When Drew turned toward her and caught her staring, she knew she still had an undeniably sentimental expression on her face. She braced herself, waiting for him to take advantage of the situation by giving her one of his searing glances, or simply a much-too-understanding smile. Instead his gaze spread contentment and warmth through her, promising her that she was exactly where she needed to be, that she hadn't made a mistake, and that he was going to do everything in his power to prove that to her.

Startled, Taylor caught and held her breath. The promise in Drew's eyes scared her more than his kisses.

"After we eat, we can decorate the tree," Noah declared, busily making plans for the three of them, unaware of the undercurrent in the air. "And wrap the present we got for Roxie. And Taylor can read me a chapter of *Charlotte's Web*. And—"

"Whoa, buddy." Feeling a tiny bit guilty about how much of her time Taylor had given already, Drew's conscience prompted him to say, "That's going to take up most of the night. Maybe she has other plans. I know *we* want her here, but we can't be greedy. We have to let her decide." He hoped that his emphasis on "we" was not lost on Taylor.

Noah argued, "But—"

"Without jabbering at her and pressuring her." Drew neatly cut him off and gave him the raised eyebrow treatment, but also tried to silently communicate that nonverbal encouragement would be okay.

Slowly Noah's eyes widened and his mouth got round. Then he giggled. "Yes, sir!"

Taylor folded her arms across her midriff. Regardless of their promise not to pressure her, two pairs of woeful eyes immediately turned to her and waited for her answer. Noah, who was sitting on his dad's forearm, even clasped his hands together in a little prayer. "No" was on the tip of her tongue, but she wavered when his little knuckles turned white, and then Drew tipped the scale. He tried to smile indifferently as he waited, but the emotion in his eyes told her all about how he and Noah would be lonely without her, rattling around in a house that was too big for two people and just right for three.

"I don't have any plans," she heard herself say, and mentally kicked herself for her lack of willpower.

"See," Noah told his dad. "She likes us."

The rest of the evening, the grown-ups took special care not to rock the boat of camaraderie. Too much had happened too quickly, and they needed time to sort through their feelings. Noah seemed the only one completely at ease. He even laughed at his "choir" as he threaded ribbons through the holes they had made with a drinking straw before baking them.

Noah was yawning by the time they were ready to add the star to the tallest of the tree's two points. Carefully, Drew picked him up and held him. When Noah set the star atop his tree, all of them breathed a sigh of relief, and Taylor flipped off the lights, leaving the room in darkness except for the brilliance of the lights nestled in the branches.

"It's perfect, Daddy." His voice was hushed and reverent.

"Absolutely perfect."

"Look, Taylor!" Noah's soft exclamation was filled with wonder. "They really are singing."

In the dark, with only the twinkling tree lights to illuminate the room, the gingerbread men did look as if they were singing. What had been an odd collection of ornaments, bows, and popcorn garland transformed the lopsided tree into a glorious celebration of the season. Taylor hugged the moment to her heart, remembering all the Christmases of her childhood and how her mother had managed to make every tree special in the same way that Noah's gingerbread choir made this tree special.

Noah yawned again and put his head on his dad's shoulder, holding out a hand for Taylor to join him. If she'd been his mother—if they'd been a family—joining him in the circle of Drew's arms would have been the most natural thing in the world. But they weren't a family. She had no business letting Noah believe that, even unconsciously. No matter how appealing the idea suddenly was to her.

In the darkness, Drew's eyes found hers, and she forgot about what was right and what was wrong. Maybe it was a trick of the darkness, maybe it was a reflection of the tree lights, but she would have sworn she saw longing in his gaze. Maybe she simply wanted to believe that he needed her with him and Noah, as if, somehow, the moment would be incomplete if she weren't included. While every self-preservation instinct she had was screaming at her to run, she stepped closer and slipped her arm around Drew's waist as Noah laid his hand on her shoulder, completing the circle.

Outside, snow fell and the temperature dropped. The windows were even beginning to frost. But inside, the three of them were warm and content and peaceful. Soon Noah's hand fell away and his mouth hung open in his sleep.

"I think we've lost him," she whispered, and stepped back, uncertain how far to go and afraid to look at Drew. Surprisingly, the tiny circle had been more intimate than Drew's kiss, leaving her flustered and very conscious of how his body felt next to hers.

Drew stifled his first instinct, which was to pull her back into his arms. He wasn't ready to let go, but his sixth sense warned him that Taylor wasn't ready to hang on, not yet anyway. Given time, he could change that. He wasn't going to give up on the dream he had of a family and of building enough memories to last a lifetime.

"He's had a long day," Taylor said to fill the quiet that pressed in on her from all sides. "You'd better go up and put him to bed."

"Will you be here when I come down?" It was more of a challenge than a question.

Not trusting her voice, Taylor nodded, reminding herself that she was staying to talk about Noah, not to spend time alone with his father. Drew left her, and before she was ready, he was coming back down the stairs. The ceiling light was still off. He didn't bother to turn it on when he walked in.

"That was quick," she murmured to make conversation.

He shrugged. "All I did was pull his shoes off and cover him up."

"You could have taken your time," she protested.

"I wasn't sure you'd still be here if I gave you a chance to slip away."

"I told you I'd stay."

Instead of approaching her, Drew headed for the window, pretending to check the snowfall. She was too defensive. Even in the semidarkness he could feel her wariness, and he hated it. He looked out at the night for a long time, watching patches of ice sparkle in the moonlight. When he couldn't delay any longer, he said, "We need to talk."

"I know. About Noah."

He pushed off with his shoulder and walked toward her. "About a lot of things."

"Noah first." She tried to sound firm, but she sounded apprehensive instead. Scrambling for the couch only made her misgivings about controlling herself more obvious. In her ears she sounded like a gawky, shy teenager when she asked, "Shouldn't we turn on a light?"

"I can see you just fine," Drew said softly as he joined her by the unlit fireplace. He settled on the love seat across from her and stretched his legs out in front of him, angling them beneath the corner of the coffee table. "Besides, I like the way the tree looks all lit up in the darkness."

"You don't think Noah was disappointed?"

"I think Noah likes the tree almost as much as he likes you."

She laughed. "Noah would like anyone who spent this much time with him, especially a woman. Kids are genetically programmed to look for mommy substitutes. It's not me," she assured him, and more importantly herself. "It's anyone in a skirt."

"He's never seen you in a skirt."

"You know what I mean!"

"No, I don't. What I know is that my son has excellent taste in women." He sat forward, bracing his elbows on his knees and clasping his hands between them. Now that his eyes had fully adjusted to the dark, he could see how tired and on edge she was. Noah wasn't the only one who'd had a long day. "I haven't really thanked you yet, Taylor, for what you did for us today. I want to—"

"Don't," Taylor interrupted. She didn't want thanks. Whatever she'd done, she'd done for herself because she wanted them to be all right. So she could walk away. Holding her hand up, she shook her head at him. "Don't."

"Don't what?" He was almost angry. "Don't say 'thank you'? Don't apologize? Don't admit that I was a jerk? Don't admit that I scared the hell out of my son?"

"Don't carry guilt around like pocket change," she told him bluntly as she dragged a hand through her hair, pulling it away from her face and holding it at the nape of her neck. "You made a mistake; you're not perfect. Don't make a federal case out of it. Let it go. Everything turned out all right."

"Because you were here, not because of anything I did. I think that stings more than the rest. Knowing you could do what I couldn't. Knowing Noah instinctively wanted you, trusted you instead of me."

"He was scared," she tried to explain, and then wished she hadn't said anything at all.

Drew's head snapped up, and his words were harsh and cold as he asked, "Don't you think I know that? Do you think I'll ever forget that?"

She didn't answer because there was no answer, no way to take away the pain he'd feel every time he remembered Noah's desperate plea or the way he'd held out his arms to her. It was an image that Drew would carry with him for a long time, and nothing she could say would change it.

"I'm sorry, Taylor. I'm sorry." Drew slumped against the couch, disgusted with himself. She didn't deserve his anger, not after all she'd done for him. "Isn't this a helluva start on fatherhood? I moved back here, determined to give my son the childhood I never had, and I begin by terrifying him, and then I move right along to yelling at you."

Heaving himself up, he paced a couple of steps to the fireplace. He wished for a fire, for some heat that could warm the cold inside him. He leaned on the mantel and was as honest as he knew how to be. "I've never been very good at loving anyone. I sure didn't learn how at home, and Lord knows I made mistakes with Anna, but I thought it would be different with Noah. I never knew it was going to be this hard or going to hurt this much."

"Maybe that's because you're asking too much of yourself," she suggested, and barely stopped herself from going to him.

Watching him hurt was as bad as watching Noah hurt, only with Noah she didn't have to censor her urge to comfort; she didn't have to sit idly by and watch the pain for fear that comfort would turn into something more. Drew was as vulnerable as she'd ever seen him, but she didn't dare touch him. All she could do was offer encouragement.

"Give yourself some time, Drew. You and Noah are both adjusting. Give him time to learn the limits of your love."

"There aren't any."

"That's what he has to learn." She took a deep breath, uncertain how to tell him about Noah's fears, but knowing that she had to. Putting it off would only make it worse. "Your son has to learn that he doesn't have to be perfect."

Drew tilted his head, staring at her intently, uneasiness tickling the hairs on the back of his neck. "What do you mean?"

"He's been so quiet and . . . so careful because his mother told him that if—" She hesitated, trying to think of a way to soften the blow, but there was none, so the words came out in a rush. "She said if he was bad, you'd give him away."

"Oh my God." Drew's knees actually buckled for a moment.

"That's why he was so terrified when you said . . ." She trailed off, unable to finish, but finishing wasn't necessary. He understood exactly what she was trying to tell him.

Drew closed his eyes and tried to fight back the rage that threatened to consume him. His hands closed around the mantel, and he pushed against it. How could Anna have done that to her own son? How could he not have known? How could he not have guessed?

Slowly he opened his eyes, and without looking at Taylor he said, "You knew. Even before he told you, you knew."

"I didn't know."

He looked at her then. She was a lousy liar, even in the dark. "You knew."

"Not for certain. I suspected maybe."

Now he was facing her, with one hand on a hip and the other still gripping the mantel. "Why in God's name didn't you tell me?"

"Tell you what exactly?" she asked sarcastically. " 'Excuse me, Drew, but I think your son is too perfect'? It was a feeling. Nothing else."

"How long did it take you to get that feeling?" When she remained silent, he raised his voice slightly and asked again. *"How long?"*

Angry herself now, she pushed up off the couch, matching him glare for glare. "What does it matter?"

Drew whistled softly as if impressed. "That long, huh?"

He tried to come to terms with the knowledge that she'd probably known from the moment she laid eyes on Noah. He made a sound that was more huff than laugh. "You should be the parent, not me."

"No."

He gave her a hard look then, struck by something that had been nagging him without his even realizing it. "Why the hell aren't you married, Taylor? Why don't you have ten kids of your own?"

"No one in their right mind would have ten kids in today's economy." she joked.

Drew didn't even smile as he crossed his arms. "Wrong answer. And that still doesn't explain why you've never been married."

"You make that sound like there are men beating down my door."

"Any man with breath in his body would want you."

Snapping her fingers, she quipped, "Breathing! I knew I was forgetting something."

"Yeah, like how to answer the question. Why is someone with your gift of nurturing still unattached?" He walked to the corner of the room and turned on a lamp. As the soft light streamed into the room, he spread his arms. "Case in point. Look at this place. Yesterday it was a very pretty house. Today it's home."

"Today it's a wreck," she informed him, pointing out the gingerbread crumbs on the table; bags and ornament boxes stacked in a chair; and the bits of popcorn left on the floor from where they'd turned over the bowl. "And the kitchen is even worse. I hope you don't expect me to clean it up. I don't do windows either."

"You don't do windows," mused Drew as he studied her, "but you care about people. Windows are a helluva lot easier than people. It doesn't make sense, Mouse."

"You don't actually believe that life is supposed to make sense, do you?" she asked, with a mocking laugh. "You've lived out there in the real world. You know better than that. Life is one practical joke after another. Haven't you noticed?"

He ignored her flippant remark. Her eyes were too bright, her laugh too forced. It was all smoke and mirrors, her way of distracting him from the real issue, the question she was trying to avoid. He narrowed his eyes and came to a conclusion. "There isn't a doubt in my mind."

"About what?" she asked suspiciously.

"That sometime . . . somewhere . . . somebody proposed. And you said no. All I want to know is, why?"

Everyone has a moment of truth, and Taylor knew hers had arrived. And she wasn't ready. She didn't want to say the words out loud, which didn't make any sense at all. After all these years, why was she so afraid to admit she wanted a life of her own? *Because maybe she didn't anymore.*

"Taylor?" He took a step toward her, and she backed up. Swearing, Drew stopped instantly and held his hands up, palms out. In a rough voice he said, "Don't back away from me. I'm not sure I can handle terrifying two people in one day."

The controlled emotion in his voice brought her up short. She realized what her actions must have looked like to him. "You've got it all wrong, Drew. You don't scare me, at least not the way you think."

"Like hell I don't," he bit out. "Not that I blame you. I'm not too sure I'd trust me either. Not after today."

"You, I trust. I'm not so sure about me though," she said quietly, so quietly that Drew wasn't entirely certain she'd spoken until she continued. "I'm having a little trouble remembering to keep my distance. I backed up because you're one of the good guys, and the way you make me feel scares me. I don't want to feel like this."

"Like what?"

"Like I might be getting attached."

"Why would that be so horrible?" he asked, confused. "I'm already way past attached."

"Because you have baggage."

Startled, he almost laughed. "Baggage? At our age, everyone has baggage. All that *baggage* is what makes us who we are. Some of us just pack lighter."

He didn't get it, she realized. She was going to have to spell it out. Lord, she hated this, hated trying to explain, but she didn't have a choice. They couldn't go on playing with fire. At least she couldn't. It was better to put all her cards on the table and have it over with.

Nervously she paced the room, ending up by the windows, closer to him. She and Drew were like book-ends bracketing the clear panes, totally aware of each other yet looking into the night. Taking a deep breath, she let it out slowly, then said, "You have Noah."

"*I have Noah?*" A shiver finger-walked up his spine as he reached out and circled her arm, swinging her around to face him.

Moonlight glinted off her blond hair and caressed her face. She looked miserable and gorgeous, all at once. The combination warned him not to jump to con-clusions. "Having Noah doesn't change what's going on between us."

"That's where you're wrong. It changes everything. You and Noah are a package deal. You said it yourself—having a child trust you is the scariest thing in the world. So you should understand why I don't want to do this anymore. I don't want to raise another family. I don't want to get attached to you."

Shocked, his fingers bit into the flesh of her arms as he stared down at her, trying to understand how he'd misread her signals. Dreams he didn't even know he had dissolved under the weight of her confession. How could she kiss him the way she had and talk about not getting attached? How could she respond to Noah so instinctively and not want children? How could he have fallen in love with the wrong woman again?

But she didn't feel wrong; she felt right. She always had.

He searched her eyes, looking for answers and find-ing none. He almost believed her until she dropped her gaze. Then he knew. She was still hiding something, something that worried her more than Noah. Inexplicably, a weight lifted from Drew's heart, and he remembered—*Nothing I can have.* If the secret to loving someone was giving more than he took, then he'd just have to find out what she wanted and give it to her.

"Good try, but you never could fool me, Mouse."

Jerking away, she said, "I wasn't trying to fool anyone. I was trying to be honest."

"Like I said, it was a good try. As far as it went." He was talking to her back because she was busy looking around the floor for the boots she'd taken off earlier. "If you don't want a family, what do you want, Taylor? What are you afraid I can't give you?"

NINE

Taylor froze. The question reached way down inside her and turned over a rock in her soul. Whether by chance or luck, he'd hit a nerve. She could feel Drew gazing at her like a wolf watching a straying lamb— confident but always hungry, and always waiting for one foolish move.

Forcing herself to action, she picked up her suede boots from where she'd dropped them near the dining room table. Only after she pulled them on did she trust herself to face him. From across the room she could feel the tension build between them as he waited patiently, his attention never wavering. He had all the time in the world, and he expected an answer.

Her chin came up; her hands fisted at her sides. "What you can't give me is certainty."

"I don't understand."

"It's very simple. If I let myself get involved with you, I'll never be certain."

"Of what?" he demanded.

"Of whether you want me for yourself or if you want me for Noah."

The moment she said it, Drew felt like he'd been sucker punched. The hell of it was, he couldn't defend himself. What he felt for her was all mixed up with what he wanted for Noah. He shoved his fingers through his hair and tried to separate one from the other.

Taylor was warm, tender, funny, gorgeous, compassionate. Sure, he wanted her for Noah, but he wanted her for himself more. He had wanted her for himself long before Noah arrived, long before he had any business thinking about waking up with her. Not that he had a prayer in hell of convincing her with a simple declaration. He'd try, but Taylor had always judged people by their actions, not their promises. Inwardly he cringed. So far he'd given her plenty of reason to believe that he was using her as a surrogate mother for Noah.

Making a decision, he said, "Then we only have one problem."

"And what's that?" she asked uneasily. He was on the move, heading for her. He looked determined.

"Getting you used to the idea."

"What idea?"

"That I want you for me." He took advantage of the fact that he'd flustered her to guide her a few steps backward. "I want you. I have wanted you. I will want you. In every tense, in every sense of the word." He stopped and drawled in mock surprise, "Oh my. Look at that. You're under the mistletoe."

Oh, Lord, that's the last place on earth you need to be, she warned herself. Drew considered mistletoe a license to steal kisses, and in turn, those potent kisses stole her resolve. Stepping back, she said, "But not for long. I try to learn from my mistakes so I can stay out of trouble."

"Then how about one for the road?" Drew didn't wait for an answer. He caught her by the elbow and pulled her close, his hands already tugging her shirt from her jeans when his mouth found hers.

He couldn't tell if the sound she made when he cupped her breast was caused by shock, pleasure, anticipation, or a combination of all three. Her softness filled his hand, teasing his senses as she pressed into his palm, then pulled away, as if she couldn't make up her mind. Her bra must have been made of gossamer and air, because it felt like nothing was between his thumb and the emerging peak.

Kissing her wasn't enough for Drew. He let his mouth trail down her throat as he ran a hand over her hip, along the back of her thigh. In one smooth motion he flexed his knees, hooked her leg, and brought it up around his thigh, opening her to the stroke of his arousal as he straightened. Slowly he let the stressed front of his fly rub against the heat hidden beneath her jeans.

Taylor caught her breath as denim scraped against denim, unexpectedly sensual, unexpectedly frustrating. The touch was a pale imitation of an intimate act, but effective nonetheless, making her conscious of the ways her body would fit more perfectly with his. Instinctively she angled her hips, and Drew responded, pushing against her again. The ashes of the fire she'd managed to control earlier began to glow, spreading a warm need through her.

With one hand wrapped around her, supporting her, and the other cradling her knee, Drew used his leverage to guide her body so they could both get as close as they could to what they really wanted. The house was still around them, and all he could hear was the sound of their uneven breathing as he thrust against her. Needing to get closer, Drew swore softly and took his hands from her long enough to dispose of his sweater and T-shirt. Her eyes widened, her mouth slightly parted as she looked at him.

Taylor knew she was staring, but she couldn't help herself. Old fantasies and the persistent pulse between her legs robbed her of the ability to move. Smooth, dark hair covered his chest and swirled around his nipples, arrowing downward over his washboard stomach, then narrowing to a fine line that disappeared into his jeans. Her gaze followed its concealed trail downward.

"You really shouldn't look at me like that, Mouse," he warned softly. A second later he grabbed her wrist. He pulled her toward the kitchen table, swung her up on it, and positioned himself intimately between her thighs.

They were still denim to denim, but somehow this position satisfied Taylor more. Her hands were free to roam over his stomach, to soak up the texture of crisp hair and tense muscles. The narrowing band of hair enticed her to roam lower.

She was functioning on instinct alone, all rational

thought having flown the moment her palms touched his hot skin. She'd never been kissed by a man who could make her forget the world so completely. She wasn't ready to stop yet or think about the consequences.

Drew brought her close again, savoring the feel of her, the soft cotton of her shirt as she pressed against him, the way her breasts molded to him, a preview of what it would be like when he brought them together—skin to skin. Her hands traveled up his abdomen and insinuated themselves between their bodies. When her fingertips toyed with his nipples, he stopped nuzzling her neck and rested his forehead against hers. He dug his hands into her hair, in a futile attempt to keep himself still and let her explore.

The way she plucked at the sensitive nubs destroyed all his good intentions. Grabbing the bottom of her shirt, he pulled it over her head and flicked open the front clasp of her bra, driven by a need to explore her body in the same way. As he peeled back the thin silk cups and exposed her, she sucked in a breath that did more to arouse him than give him pause. His fingertips traced the line of her collarbone as he allowed himself to look his fill.

Silently he enjoyed her, smoothing his hand over the top of her breast and under to cup the soft mound, to lift it as he began to lower his head. Pleasure pooled in his belly when she dragged in a shuddering breath and wove her fingers into his hair. He traced the outer edge of her nipple with his tongue, and, to him, it seemed as though he had wanted to taste her forever.

She arched her back in a clear signal that she wanted him to take more than a taste.

A second before his mouth closed on her, Drew heard footsteps clumping down the stairs and Noah's voice as he descended. "Daddy?"

His heart literally stopped, and Taylor whispered, "Oh my God!" If the situation hadn't been so desperate, he might have laughed, but he didn't have time. His only thought was to protect Taylor and Noah from embarrassment, which meant he had to intercept Noah and give Taylor time to recover.

"Don't worry," he told her as he sprinted for the dining room. En route to Noah, he flipped on the kitchen light and snatched up his sweater. He was dressed and skidding into the archway by the time Noah appeared. Only slightly out of breath, he managed, "Here I am."

Noah yawned. "I got up to go to the bathroom. You weren't in your room."

"Taylor and I were in the kitchen. Cleaning up!" he added swiftly as he saw his son open his mouth to ask the inevitable question. The faint clatter of dishes being stacked emanated from the kitchen. Noah peeked around his dad, who said, "Hey, you! It's way past your bedtime. You go on back up and get into your pajamas. I'll be up to tuck you in as soon as we're through in the kitchen."

Sighing but turning around to obey, Noah said, "Tell Taylor I like the tree."

"I sure will," Drew promised.

"Tell her we won't forget about helping her tomorrow."

"That too."

Noah stopped. "And tell her she smells good, better even than Roxie."

Drew laughed and herded his son toward the stairs. "Trust me, son. I will tell her." Under his breath he said, "If she's still speaking to me when I get back to the kitchen."

When his son had mounted the stairs and disappeared around the corner and into his room, Drew dropped his head onto the newel post and let the pent up tension escape from his body. Man was not meant to change gears so swiftly. Or so often. He raised up and looked at the kitchen warily.

Noah's timing couldn't have been worse. Taylor wasn't the kind of woman who climbed in and out of men's beds, and he had no doubt that the passion between them—how close they'd come to making love— scared her. She always gave more than she took, and he suspected that was true of her in bed. She'd give all of herself, and she'd have a hard time walking away afterward.

In fact, he was counting on it. Every cell in his body promised him that once he was inside her, something special would happen, something that would create a bond between them. He needed that physical bond. He needed every advantage he could get. All he had were five short days until Christmas, and something told him that he'd better make the most of them.

Taylor was still busily cleaning up when he stuck his

head in the kitchen. Her back was to him as he said, "You can stop now. The coast is clear."

"For the moment," she said, and turned around. She wasn't prepared for the sudden rush of excitement that ripped through her as she faced him. His hair was mussed; his lips were sexy and swollen, and his sweater was on wrong side out—all reminders of what they'd been doing and how close they'd come to being discovered. How close she'd come to making a fatal mistake.

With a hand on her hip and a vague gesture toward the table, she asked, "Do you have any idea how irresponsible that was?"

"Do you have any idea how incredibly beautiful you are?

"I'm serious, Drew."

He raised his eyebrows and sank a shoulder into the door frame. "So am I. Very serious. I still want you, Taylor. An interruption's not going to change that. I don't think I've ever wanted another woman more. Certainly not the way I want you."

Such dangerous words, she thought, so sincere. They were dangerous because she wanted to believe them, and so sincere that her pulse raced with the possibilities.

Being with them during the last two days had confused her, made her question her choices. Everything that should have been a chore was a joy. Holding Noah had aroused feelings she'd thought long dead and buried. She had forgotten how much she loved children, how easily they could make you feel alive and loved. Touching Drew brought out new emotions that were just as strong, just as treacherous, and more difficult to control. She had to deny them, or lose herself.

"But I don't want you," she finally said, but the emotional tug-of-war inside her was far from over. Her declaration was too weak, too late.

Drew had watched all the doubts rush through her, clouding the issue of what she wanted and bringing sadness to her eyes. Gently he suggested, "Maybe you don't know what you want."

She pushed her sleeves up, the sadness replaced with a militant light. "Yes I do. I want my freedom. I've spent thirteen years taking care of people. I don't want to do that anymore. I've got other plans for my life. You and Noah are not what I want."

"Then maybe we're what you *need*," he told her softly, because he believed it. She needed someone who'd take care of her for a change, someone who'd value her touch. She needed someone who wanted all that passion she kept bottled up inside. She needed someone to love her. Drew thought he and Noah were the right men for all those jobs.

"You're wrong about that too," she argued more calmly than she felt.

"I don't think so." Drew resorted to fighting dirty— she left him no choice really. He flicked a gaze over her body, pausing at the juncture of her thighs and letting himself remember how she responded to his touch. "I think I'm exactly what you need."

Then his gaze made a slow journey upward. He locked eyes with her, knowing that desire and remembrance would be written all over his face. "And *that* I know for a fact."

Heat flamed her cheeks, and Taylor almost succumbed to the urge to throw something. Preferably at his head. Lord, he was arrogant. And he was right, she admitted unhappily. If you ignored your hormones for too long, they mutinied, and hers had been in full revolt. She hadn't had a rational thought in her head. That was an understatement actually. She'd been half-naked on the kitchen table, and if Noah hadn't interrupted, she would have been completely naked on the kitchen table in a matter of minutes.

However, she was thinking more clearly now. She'd had a reprieve, and she intended to make the most of it. As she passed him on her way to get her coat, she said, "All you're talking about is sex. In my experience I've found that sex is like an itch. If you don't scratch it, it'll go away." She hauled open the closet door and retrieved her coat. Then she flashed him a determined look. "I certainly won't be scratching. And *that* I know for a fact."

Unruffled, Drew took her coat out of her grasp, holding it up for her to put on. As she turned around to slip her arms in, he lowered his head close to her ear and said, "Based on my experience, which is probably wider than yours, sex is like one of those Christmas snow globes. Everything looks so peaceful. All the snow is settled in artful drifts around the figurines."

He paused to settle the coat over her shoulders, his voice drifting into a seductive rasp that held her motionless. "Doesn't look like it's ever going to snow again inside that globe. Then someone turns it over, and the storm begins. Sometimes even the tiniest bump will make the snow swirl up. So quick, so intense, almost blinding."

She began to sag and caught herself. Jerking away from his hands, she adjusted the collar of her coat and dug the keys out of the pocket. "Thanks for the warning. From now on I'll be careful not to bump into you."

Chuckling, Drew held the door open. "That's going to be kind of hard. You promised Noah we could help clean up the float tomorrow. What did you say? The high school, about ten o'clock? Then there's the Christmas caroling around the neighborhood the day after tomorrow."

After narrowing her eyes and pressing her lips together, Taylor walked away without saying a word. He watched her until she got in her car and drove off. Then he shut the door and said, "Taylor Marie Bishop, I'm going to do my best to turn you over and shake you up."

He took the stairs two at a time and whistled all the way to Noah's room.

Without opening her eyes, Taylor snaked a hand out from underneath the covers and fumbled around for the ringing telephone. When her hand found the receiver, she lifted it and then hung it up. Only one person could possibly be calling her this early, and she didn't feel up to dueling metaphors at dawn. Maybe he'd take the hint.

He didn't.

With a sigh, Taylor opened her eyes and reached for the phone again, intending to repeat the procedure. However, the instant she raised the receiver she heard Drew's frenzied *"Don't hang up!"*

Bolting upright, she brought the phone to her ear. "Drew? What's wrong?"

"I need help. Look, I didn't know who else to call." He sounded like a man at the end of a very short rope. "Noah won't eat his breakfast."

Taylor pulled the receiver away from her ear and looked at it as though it might be defective. Surely she couldn't have heard right. Shaking her head to clear the cobwebs left from a bad night's sleep, she said heavily, "You called me at—" she had to look at the alarm, "six-thirty in the morning and woke me up because Noah won't eat his Post Toasties?"

"No, because Noah won't eat his Cocoa Puffs."

"Oh, well, that makes it better!"

"This is serious, Taylor."

Something in his voice straightened her spine and made her grip the phone tighter. "Okay, tell me."

The silence on the other end of the phone indicated he was thinking, obviously trying to figure out how to phrase the situation. "This isn't like Noah. He's sitting in there staring at the table, with his arms crossed and refusing to eat a bite."

"Did he tell you why?"

"He says—and I quote—'You can't make me eat breakfast.' The weird thing is that breakfast is the only meal he likes. Cocoa Puffs every day of the week wasn't my idea! It's the only thing he likes. He eats them and a piece of fruit every morning. Day in and day out. It's like a ritual around here."

"Did you use a different bowl or something?"

"Nope."

"Run out of fruit?"

"Nope."

"Did *anything* unusual happen this morning?"

She could hear him as he exhaled. "No, nothing. I called him for breakfast. Started my coffee. He was a little slow, so I called him again—"

"Do you usually have to call him twice?"

"No."

"Then the light is dawning." Taylor chuckled.

"Care to shine some of it this way?"

Lounging back against the headboard, Taylor said, "Life as you know it is about to come to an end. Your patience is about to be stretched to the limit."

"Spill it, Taylor. What do you know that I don't know?"

"I know that your son trusts you enough to test you. He's trying to figure out if you really meant that part about never trading him in. Be thankful he didn't test you by letting the bathtub overflow . . . although," she added thoughtfully, "that could be next."

Stunned silence followed her pronouncement. Then he asked, "What am I supposed to do?"

"Depends on what you have already done." When he didn't volunteer anything, she took a guess. "By any chance did you tell him, in a big bad voice, that he had to sit there until he finished?"

"Uh . . . I may have said something like that."

Poor Drew, she thought, and not for the first time. "So what did he do?"

"Crossed his arms and slumped back in his chair. And told me I couldn't make him eat breakfast."

Taylor clapped her hand over her mouth to stifle a laugh. She could visualize Drew's shocked face as sweet, angelic Noah turned into a stubborn little devil. After politely clearing her throat, she dispensed advice. "Well, first of all, never, ever make threats about food. It's dumb, and unnecessary. Put good food in front of him and he'll eat when he's hungry. I've never seen a kid choose starvation over a full tummy. Not for long anyway.

"Second of all, never make threats that end up punishing *you*. When you go back to work, you can't wait all day for him to finish breakfast. And lastly, when necessary . . . cheat."

"Cheat?"

"You go back in there, smile, tell him he's finished, and excuse him from the table."

"What about wasting the cereal? What about the mandatory starving-children-in-America speech?"

"Pour the cereal down the drain, and send a check to the Hope Foundation. Let Noah help you mail it, and tell him what it's for. No lectures."

"Just like that?"

"Just like that."

"Taylor," he admitted reverently, "I need to have you on twenty-four-hour call."

"That's called a mother, and I'm not interested." With exaggerated care, Taylor hung up the phone and tried to hold on to her temper.

Drew heard the click a second before her words sank in. And by then it was too late. She was gone; redialing would be useless. By the time he could punch in the number, she'd have either unhooked the cord or turned off the ringer.

Dammit! He banged the phone down and leaned back in the leather chair. Unspoken recriminations echoed in the study as he rubbed the bridge of his nose. How could he have been so stupid? Why hadn't he simply thanked her for the advice and left it at that? The comment wasn't even about her! It was more about his feelings of inadequacy as a parent. Not that Taylor would believe him.

Why should she? From the very first he'd done nothing but sing her praises as a holiday organizer and beg for her help with Noah. He hadn't even asked her for an old-fashioned no-kid-in-sight date. Well, he'd remedy that situation today. Regardless of the fact they were way past the getting-to-know-you garbage, a date might change her mind about his motives.

With one crisis behind him, he looked ahead to the next and smiled. His son trusted him enough to misbehave. He could handle that. Then he'd handle Taylor. She could hang up on him, but she couldn't get rid of him.

TEN

Taylor bent down to add her presents to the neatly wrapped packages spilling out from under the perfectly symmetrical evergreen. Although Martha had painstakingly trimmed the tree, Taylor wasn't sure she liked the results. All the homemade ornaments were on the back and sides, while the glittery, store-bought decorations were displayed on the front. When she straightened, her dad wandered into the room and draped an arm over her shoulders, keeping her company while she studied the tree.

"Don't think we ever had one that wasn't tied to the wall," he said. His reading glasses hung around his neck, and he had on a purple cardigan sweater and gold shirt in deference to the school's colors. "That Martha has an eye for trees. She went all the way into Morriston for this one."

"Mmm," Taylor said. It was an elegant tree, but it wasn't special. It didn't have a gingerbread choir. It didn't tug at her heart the way Noah's did.

As always, her dad's radar picked up on her emotions, and he gave her a comforting squeeze. "Everybody's got their own way, Taylor Marie. You should have seen her putting on the ornaments. She must have spent the whole day yesterday. Arranging and rearranging the thing till she was satisfied. Asked Clay's opinion so many times, I thought he might strangle her."

Taylor chuckled. She knew better than to ask any of the Bishop men their opinion about fashion, decoration, or haircuts. "Poor Martha. I feel terrible. I should have warned her."

Her father looked at her blankly. "What for? Clay told her it looked fine. Every time she asked."

Reaching up to her shoulder, Taylor patted her father's hand. "If that's all he said, then it was a miracle that *she* didn't strangle *him*."

"That reminds me. How are you making out with Drew?"

Taylor swallowed at her dad's innocent choice of words. "Uh . . . fine. The house is decorated, and their tree's up. I've promised to take them Christmas caroling, but for the most part I'm done with him—I mean them. That means you'll finally be seeing more of me around here, and Martha won't have to do so much."

"Don't you worry about that. Martha is almost as crazy about this holiday as you are. The only thing she hasn't done is put your box on the tree. She thought you might want to do that yourself, since Clay's been telling her how you are about Christmas."

"The star! It's in my box!" Taylor gasped as she realized what was missing from the tree. She'd been so busy with Drew and Noah that she'd forgotten all about it.

"She made do." He pointed at the top of the tree. "Clay bought her that angel. He says he's going to buy her an angel for every year they're married. He sure is crazy about that girl. She doesn't have any family to speak of. Her parents are gone, and her brother's in the army. She and Clay plan on being here for Christmas every year."

"Every year?" Once again Taylor had to fight back the territorial impulses that welled up inside her as she realized that next year would be the same as this one. Martha would buy another perfect tree, put the prettiest decorations on the front, and put Santa on the roof instead of in the yard.

How ironic, she thought bitterly. She'd been complaining for years because nobody lifted a finger around the holidays. And now that someone had taken an interest, she wasn't sure she liked it. By buying the angel, Clay had created a new Bishop tradition and forced a changing of the guard without ever asking her permission.

And why should he have? she asked herself honestly. She wasn't the mother. She was only the sister. This house was as much Clay's home as it was hers. He had every right to make his wife feel welcome.

Looking up at the glorious angel crowning the tree, she knew she couldn't ruin her sister-in-law's joy by asking her to put up the star instead. No, the star would stay in the box this year, and so would her ornaments. She had Noah's tree. It was only fair that Martha had this one. She hugged her dad. Sometimes he was a very wise man, even when he was trying very hard to disguise advice as idle conversation.

"You know, Dad, I think the angel looks a little like Momma."

"So do you, baby, so do you." He kissed the top of her head. "Ready to get the float in shape?" he asked.

Taylor punched him playfully. "You better hope it's already in shape. We don't have much time to fix anything that's broken. The parade's on Thursday."

"Today's Tuesday," he said. "We have plenty of time."

"Ha!" she scoffed. "That's what you think."

"It ain't over till the man blows the whistle."

By rote she added, "And even then you can nudge the football forward a few inches."

They smiled at each other and headed for the high school.

As Taylor followed her dad's car into the school parking lot, Clay leaned forward from the back seat to peer out the windshield. "Good Lord! What's wrong with David! He's here on time."

"He's suffering from fear," Martha explained. "Taylor threatened to take all his stickers off the antiques if he was late."

"And I meant it." Taylor chuckled as she thought of David's face when she had issued her ultimatum. "If

Tim can store the float in his barn all year, the least David can do is haul the thing over here."

The job of spit-polishing the float was hard enough without having to work in the cold, and the large corrugated metal building, which served as the high school's auto shop, provided heat and plenty of light. Her dad wheeled his car into position beside the short flatbed trailer, which was topped with an odd collection of primary-colored "machinery" that transformed the trailer into a toy factory. Wisely Taylor parked her car as far away as possible from David and the float. She wasn't sure how good her brother was at backing flatbed trailers into shop bays or how much room he'd need to maneuver his monster truck.

The rest of this year's cleanup crew stood around on the cold asphalt, stamping their feet and waiting for Coach Bishop to unlock the doors. The clump of people waved at them, more people than Taylor ever remembered coming down to help with the float. Of course, her comparison was probably jaded by last year's turnout of only four people.

"Well, look who's waiting on you, Taylor!" Martha said coyly, drawing her attention to a figure that stood head and shoulders above the rest. "Now, that's what I call devotion. The man's come all the way down here to help us scrub and touch up the paint on this dirty old float. Then again, why wouldn't he hightail it down here to get on your good side? You're a mighty good catch for a man with a small child to raise."

Taylor stiffened. After this morning's conversation with Drew, she knew very well that her appeal for him was her maternal qualities. Having Martha point out the obvious was an extra dose of unwanted reality.

To her total surprise and amazement, Clay said, "Nah, honey, Drew and Taylor go way back. Before Noah. My old buddy might be trying to impress her, but I doubt it's for Noah's sake." He opened his door and stuck a leg out. "Little sister, you be careful you don't break his heart. I wouldn't take that too kindly."

"Wait a minute!" Taylor objected. "Aren't you supposed to be protecting me and saying that to him?"

"I already did. About thirteen years ago."

Nonplussed, Taylor sat in the car several seconds after they got out, replaying her brother's revelations in her mind. Yeah, well, she warned herself before she got too sentimental, it didn't matter how Drew felt back then. Thirteen years ago Drew didn't have a child. Thirteen years ago she didn't feel as if she were on parole and that one false move would take away her freedom.

Although Drew and Noah were ten or fifteen feet away, seeing them had the same unsettling impact on her as yesterday. They scared the hell out of her. *I deserve a life*, she reminded herself. She'd been on her own for less than a year. She wasn't ready to fall in love, wasn't ready to be a wife—much less a mother.

When Noah came running up to the side of her car and opened the door, his baby-tooth smile lit up her heart like a pinball machine and sounded every self-preservation warning she had. Drew was a package deal, and if she wasn't careful, she'd find herself falling in love with the package.

"We were the first ones here. Daddy said it was important to be on time so you wouldn't worry about us. He said you especially needed our help because you don't get enough help." A little disappointment crept into his tone. "But you've got lots of helpers here. Can I still help?"

"You'd better. I'm counting on you."

He smiled again and moved back so she could get out. "We've been waiting with the cheer girls, and they say I can be a mascot. What's a mascot?"

"Well . . ." She thought about a definition while she shut the door. "It's kind of like a lucky charm for the football team."

"Would I get to wear a uniform?"

Drew came up behind his son in time to hear the last question. "Sorry, buddy, I don't think the team has a jersey that small."

"Of course they do," Taylor corrected instantly. Even with Noah separating them, Drew was too close. Disagreeing with Drew was her way of putting at least some verbal distance between them. "Well, *we* have one, in the attic . . . somewhere. I'm sure of it."

"Daddy, can I go tell them I have a uniform?"

Horrified, Taylor realized that if Noah left, she'd be alone with Drew. She wasn't ready to reopen last night's conversation or discuss why she'd hung up on him this morning. So she quickly offered, "I'll go with him."

Before Drew could answer, a pretty blond teenager got his attention by waving. She pointed at Noah and then to herself in a gesture that indicated she wanted

Noah to come back over. She even started toward them, intending to meet him halfway.

One side of Drew's mouth crooked up in a smile. "Well, buddy, since Stephanie seems to like having you around, I guess you can go tell her about the uniform."

"She says our hair is the same color," Noah confided before he walked away. To the adults' credit, neither of them laughed until Noah was out of earshot.

"Ooh, are you going to be in trouble when that kid gets older! He's already got cheerleaders eating out of the palm of his hand."

"Maybe I should ask for some pointers," he said.

"Why?" Taylor quipped. "As I recall, you had your share of cheerleaders chasing after you."

"I'm out of practice."

"Ha!"

"Well, what would you call it? My technique definitely seems to be slipping. Last night I had the woman of my dreams literally in the palm of my hand, but she *slipped* through my fingers."

His teasing tone was at odds with the martial light in his eyes, a light that promised her it wouldn't happen again. Taylor wondered if he'd lain awake tossing and turning last night as she had. If he'd kicked off the covers in frustration despite the chill in the house as she had. Or punched the pillow and counted wolves in sheep's clothing in a desperate attempt to get some sleep. No, he looked too rested for any of that. He'd probably spent last night happily dreaming—

Suddenly she felt hot again, flustered. And susceptible to his charm. What Clay had said about warning

Drew not to break her heart thirteen years ago was still fresh in her mind, clouding her judgment. As a safety precaution, she made up an excuse about needing to talk to her father and silently swore she'd spend the rest of the day as far away from Drew as possible.

As far as possible wasn't far enough. When she glanced up to ask for a second opinion on a loose piece of carpet, Drew caught her gaze instantly, like a falcon spotting its prey. He wouldn't let her go, holding her attention with the same hungry stare she remembered from last night. The look passing between them was a sexual tug-of-war, a close encounter of the sensual kind.

Scraping up every ounce of willpower, Taylor closed her eyes, turned her back, and hollered, "Hey, David, come over here and look at this!"

A short while later, she knew Drew wasn't going to let her ignore him. He slipped up beside her. Sighing, she looked around for moral support and found none. Everyone was busy with their own project. Having already learned her lesson about looking directly at him, Taylor stared at the floor as she said, "I don't have time for this, Drew."

"That's all right. I can get the hammer myself."

Amusement laced his voice as he put one hand at her waist to steady her and leaned past her to retrieve the tack hammer she'd been using to refasten the carpet. While his actions gave the appearance of being a perfectly innocent touch, his hand moved upward, his fingers straying toward the underside of her breast and caressing her for a second. Taylor froze, heat rushing to her cheeks and surprise creating a forbidden thrill in her belly. Drew's fly front was pressed to her hip and scraped across it as he reached.

"Oh, sorry," he whispered against her ear. "I didn't mean to . . . bump into you."

And then he was gone, and so were her illusions about ignoring him.

By midafternoon the workers had dwindled to a hard-core few, and Taylor was ready to strangle Drew. The casual observer might think he was hard at work on the float, but Taylor knew better—he was hard at work on her. She had experienced, firsthand, the glances that were too intense to be classified as glances; the casual touches that mysteriously happened to brush erogenous zones; and the double entendres that went completely unnoticed by everyone else, yet had her on edge.

As if she'd called his name, Drew broke off a conversation and caught her staring again. He smiled before returning to his discussion with Clay.

"Daddy's smiling at us," Noah said.

"No, he was smiling at you," Taylor told him, tweaking his nose affectionately.

"No, it was both of us. He has a different smile when he sees you. He started to smile at me, but then he saw you and his smile slowed down."

Taylor snuck another look at Drew. Did he really have a different smile for her? Shamelessly she prodded Noah as he polished the dials on a piece of machinery, "What do you mean?"

"When it's only me, he smiles real quick, like he can't hold on to his smile and it gets away from him. When he smiles at you, he does it slow, like he's trying to make it last or like he's remembering secret stuff." Noah handed her the towel. "I'm done."

Numbly Taylor took the towel and helped him down from the trailer, hardly listening to him and Stephanie as her mind whirled. If there was one thing she knew, it was that kids were very difficult to fool. Children could generally see right through a person because they picked up on minute details. They still relied heavily on body language to help them understand what grown-ups wanted. If Noah said his dad had a special smile for her, then it was gospel.

Without even realizing it, Noah and Clay were doing a fine job of pleading Drew's case. It was almost as if they were saying, "Hey, what could it hurt to give the guy a chance?" She could feel a great big section of the wall around her heart crumbling and tried to shore it up.

"I don't have a bike yet," Noah explained to Stephanie. "We just moved here."

The word "bike" snared Taylor's attention. *Bike!* Her eyes widened as she realized the importance of Noah's statement. He didn't have a bike *yet.* As in, he expected one from Santa.

"Stephanie, watch Noah for a second," Taylor ordered, and made a beeline for Drew. Grabbing him by the arm, she unceremoniously pulled him away from Clay. Her voice dropped to a whisper as she said, "Bike. He wants a bike from Santa."

"Bike? I didn't get him a bike," he whispered back urgently. "It's the middle of winter, for crying out loud. I got him a sled."

"You'd better take that sled back and get him a bike pronto. The hardware store still had a couple of small red ones with training wheels when I drove by yesterday. They were in the front window."

Drew checked his watch. "I'll have to go tomorrow. They close in an hour, and I don't know if Roxie's home."

"If you wait, the bikes may be gone! Look, I'll take care of Noah." The offer popped out, and she couldn't take it back. Nor did she really want to take it back, Taylor realized. She and Noah had their own shopping to do. She had something in mind that would make walking away a little easier.

Although her offer to baby-sit tempted him, Drew was leery of accepting. He'd made so many mistakes with her, he didn't want to make another. He shook his head. "Thanks, but you've got better things to do with your time than look after Noah."

"It's the least I can do after you pitched in and worked so hard today."

"Whoa. Stop right there. You don't owe me anything. I didn't come down here to make you feel obligated. I wanted to help."

"I know," she said softly. "And so do I. It's my way of apologizing for hanging up this morning."

Drew shot a quick glance around the shop. It wasn't as crowded as before, but this wasn't the place he wanted to have this conversation. "What I said this morning—it wasn't about you, Taylor. It was frustration with myself."

Reaching up, she touched a finger to his mouth, but

quickly snatched it away as the warmth of his lips burned her finger. "Shut up before you make it worse. Besides, Noah and I have some shopping to do too. I'll bring him by when we're through."

"Wait." He fished his wallet out of his pocket. "Here's the spare key. If I'm not there, let yourself in and check with Roxie. She'll come over if she can."

"Don't worry. I've got it covered. Now go."

Surprising himself and her, he dropped a kiss on her forehead and said, "You're an angel. I owe you dinner at the fanciest restaurant in town. You can collect just as soon as I finish my baby-sitting negotiations with Stephanie."

"Pizza Hut allows children. You don't have to get a baby-sitter for Noah."

"But I don't want to take Noah. I want to take you. I want candles and wine and atmosphere. How about tomorrow night?"

Yesterday Taylor would have said no. Yesterday she still had some common sense. Today she almost said yes, until she remembered. "We're already caroling around the neighborhood."

"Thursday?"

"The Christmas Pageant at church," she said.

"Friday?"

"The parade, and—"

"Saturday's Christmas Eve," he finished. "Dammit, Taylor." He pointed a finger at her as he backed away. "I'm not giving up."

When he was out of earshot, Taylor surprised herself by whispering, "Good. 'Cause I'm not sure if I want you to."

Snowflakes were beginning to flutter down as the group of carolers strolled up Roxie's walkway. Every one of them was looking forward to the reward that awaited them only a couple of streets away—hot chocolate and an appetizing buffet. Martha swore her singing resembled the sounds made by a wounded rhino, so she had volunteered to stay home, handle the refreshments, and greet the neighbors they always invited to the annual Bishop after-caroling open house.

As tempting as the party sounded, Drew didn't think his son was going to make it, despite his determination to be a part of the festivities. For the last couple of blocks, he'd been walking with his head down, his chin buried in the opening of his coat. Seemingly oblivious to where they were, he concentrated on putting one foot in front of the other and maintained a death grip on the plush teddy bear that Taylor had given him as an early Christmas present.

"You look like one of Santa's reindeer!" Drew teased.

Noah looked at his dad. "I do?"

"Yep." Drew picked him up. "Your nose is bright red, which means I think we'd better say good-bye after we sing to Roxie."

"Bear is kind of cold," Noah admitted, referring to the newfound pal, who hadn't left his arms since yesterday.

When Drew had come home last night after buying the bike, he had found Roxie baby-sitting Noah and the new addition to the family—Bear. According to Noah, the stuffed animal was absolutely the best bear ever and, at bedtime, even rated a kiss on the nose and a pat on the head from Dad. Also according to Noah as told to him by Taylor, Bear wasn't scared of the dark, chased closet monsters away, and could always be counted upon to keep a secret. Drew smiled to himself. In addition to all of those attributes, pretty soon Bear was going to be the most traveled bear in town if Noah kept dragging him every step he took.

As Roxie opened her door, the group began to sing "Jingle Bells," which was the one song Noah could actually belt out with confidence. After they finished and waved good-bye to Roxie, Drew tapped Taylor on the shoulder and motioned toward his house next door. "I think we're going to have to go home. Bear's getting a little cold."

"Mmm," Taylor acknowledged, her teeth chattering slightly. "Smart bear. He knows when to admit he's had enough."

Drew looked at her sharply. He didn't like the fatigue he heard in her voice or the chill. They'd spent all day putting up flyers about the parade and reminding people to bring toys or canned food to put on the float as it passed. They'd walked the parade route and handled a number of last-minute details, since Taylor was unofficially in charge of the volunteer parade. They'd also helped move furniture out of the Bishop living room to make room for tonight's open house. The day had started at nine o'clock. That was twelve hours ago, and there'd hardly been a quiet moment.

"You look a little cold yourself," Drew said with a frown.

"Cold? My toes are numb."

"Then that's it." Drew whistled and raised his hand for Clay's attention. "These two need to warm up. I'll bring Taylor over when she can feel her toes again."

Clay gave a wave in return, and the group sang their way to the next house. Taylor would have argued with Drew's macho assumption that he knew what was best for her, but she wouldn't have had a leg to stand on—literally. She was about to drop. She gratefully leaned into Drew's side as he wrapped an arm around her.

"What do the two of you say to some hot chocolate?" Drew asked.

"Extra marshmallows, please," Taylor said.

"Me too," Noah seconded. "And a cup for Bear."

"And a cup for Bear," Drew echoed, feeling better than he had in a couple of days. He wasn't walking on eggshells around Noah, and Taylor had actually leaned into his embrace.

He got them inside and parked them both on the couch. By the time he'd started a fire in the fireplace, Taylor was curled up with her head on the sofa arm and out like a light. Noah sat on the other side, grinning.

He whispered, "I guess she was tireder than us."

"I guess she was," Drew whispered back. Then he laid his finger across his lips and motioned for Noah to come with him to the kitchen. After putting water on to boil for the chocolate, he went back to the living room and covered Taylor with a blanket. She'd readjusted in his absence until she lay with her head on the cushion and her hands beneath her cheek.

While he looked down at her, he reached a hand under the lampshade and quietly flipped off the light. Even asleep, without the big blue eyes dominating her face, she was gorgeous. Taking care of her could be addictive, he realized. She'd always owned a part of his heart, but now she owned a chunk of his soul, the same way Noah did. They were his first thoughts in the morning and his last at night. All his dreams of having a big family just like the Bishops disappeared. All he needed was Taylor and Noah.

On impulse, he knelt down beside her, studying her profile and tucking the soft velour blanket securely around her shoulders. He kissed the corner of her eye and whispered, "Everything's going to be okay, sweetheart. You've got me now."

Quietly he got up and headed for the phone. "No, sir, Coach Bishop, she hasn't moved a muscle. The smell of hot chocolate didn't even wake her up. . . . I don't think we should either. Let's just let her sleep till morning. Noah and I'll bring her over then. . . . No, no imposition at all. . . . Yes, sir, I'll take care of her. You don't have to worry about that."

After tucking his son in, he sat beside the fire until almost midnight, debating with himself as to whether or not to carry her to the guest room. He doubted she'd wake up. Noah never did when he was sleeping this soundly. The real reason he hesitated was his lack of faith in his own self-control. Chances were he'd never make it to the guest room.

The fire crackled loudly as he set his cup of chocolate down and decided to take his chances. She didn't need to be down here. The fire wouldn't burn all night, and in all probability the sofa would give her a stiff neck.

Carefully he lifted the blanket off, mesmerized by the curve of her waist as she lay on her side and the way her arm, which was anchored across her midriff, unconsciously plumped up her breasts. The soft knit outfit she had on hugged every swell and valley of her body. The long top was finished in points that sported tiny brass bells, and they chinked faintly as he slid his hands beneath her knees and back.

When he lifted her, she stirred and then settled her head against his chest, nuzzling until she found just the right spot for her cheek. Drew gritted his teeth. All he had on with his trousers was a T-shirt. As she exhaled a satisfied sigh, her breath warmed the cotton and his chest.

The tension in his body made carrying her more difficult, made his arms ache. Forcing himself to relax, he slowly climbed the steps, trying to keep his movements smooth and easy. The last thing his self-control needed at the moment was for Taylor to wake up, looking sexy and sleepy.

Drew soon discovered that negotiating the stairs was a piece of cake compared with opening the door to the guest room. The sharp click of the latch as he opened it seemed more like a rifle shot in the quiet house. Taylor stirred at the sound and then became so suddenly still in his arms that he knew she was awake.

For Taylor, the sharp sound finally ended the dream she'd been trying so hard to hold on to. For a split second she was tempted to ignore the noise and refuse reality, but the hard masculine pillow beneath her head forced her awake. Her eyes snapped open, and she froze.

Casting around in her mind, the last clear memory she could find was of sitting down on Drew's couch to wait for hot chocolate. She had a vague memory of being covered with a blanket, but that was it. Her consciousness narrowed to the sensations of darkness around her, soft cotton and muscle beneath her cheek, strong arms around her, and the strong quick beat of Drew's heart that duplicated the acceleration of her own. But that was the only sign he was affected by their closeness.

"You fell asleep. So I called your house, and everyone agreed it would be better to let you sleep," he explained as he let her legs slide to the ground. "This is the guest room. I was afraid you'd get a stiff neck on the couch."

Taylor kept her gaze glued to the collar of his T-shirt for fear he'd see the disappointment on her face at being put down. Somehow waking up in his arms had been so easy, as if a decision had been made for her. "I —I had a bad night last night and a long day," she apologized. "I'm sorry, I didn't mean to crash on you."

"Hey." He lifted her chin. "Don't you get it? That's what I'm here for. My only complaint is that in my dreams when you stay the night, you don't spend it in the guest room."

At his frank confession, Taylor's resolve melted. She didn't care why he wanted her, just that he did. She wanted to feel his touch and touch him in return. Knowing the answer, she asked the question anyway. For whatever reason, she wanted to hear him say the words. "In your dreams . . . where do I sleep?"

"That's just it. You don't sleep. I don't sleep." Drew still had his arms around her, and hers were nestled between them. "Not for long anyway."

Taylor closed her eyes against the wave of desire that washed over her. She wanted him to make love to her. Just this once she wanted to forget about choices and tomorrow. She wanted to forget about everything except how he made her feel inside.

Opening her eyes, Taylor said, "I don't want to sleep in the guest room." Her arms slid upward, circling his neck. "I don't think I want to sleep at all."

Almost before the words left her mouth, Drew picked her back up. He'd waited thirteen years. He didn't plan to wait another second. When he nudged his bedroom door shut with his hip, he put her down. As her feet touched the floor he reached behind him and locked it.

Leaning against it, he allowed himself to pause. He couldn't get enough of her—her scent, the softness of her hair, the way she sucked in her breath when she was excited, the way she tried not to look down as he pulled her into the cradle of his thighs. With one hand he raised her chin until her gaze was level with his. With the other he guided her hand downward, savoring the feel of her palm as it slid over his belly and cupped him.

Her eyes widened, and Drew chuckled. "Doesn't take much contact with you to get a rise out of me."

That last word was sucked back in as she moved her hand, stroking the length of his shaft through his trousers.

"Obviously not," she said, enjoying the way he surged into her hand as his mouth found hers.

The kiss foreshadowed the intimacy to come. His tongue swept deeper with each stroke, possessing her mouth, broadcasting his need to be inside her. The way she accepted his kiss communicated the same need.

Drew walked them to the bed, peeling clothes from Taylor as he went. Her panties were all that was left by the time they reached the bed. Shyly she crossed her arms across her breasts. Shaking his head, Drew pulled her arms away and shed his T-shirt.

He forced himself to go slowly. They'd been this close before. Drew remembered how she'd arched her back, presenting herself to him as his mouth almost closed over her nipple.

Taylor was remembering too. Her nipple hardened from the cool air and anticipation, but he didn't move, didn't touch her. The waiting began an insistent pulse between her legs.

When he did finally move, he pressed her back onto the bed and reached for her panties. Taylor's breath was shallow, the tension unbearable because he wouldn't release her gaze. His eyes bored into hers as his fingertips brushed against her hips, whisking down her last scrap of clothing. Then he undid his trousers and peeled down to the skin, kicking them off as he joined her on the bed.

Taylor swore she wouldn't make a sound when he finally brought their bodies together, his hardness against her belly and her breasts against the smooth pelt of hair covering his chest. But she did. The sound was more sigh than moan. The moan came next when he cupped her breast and lowered his head. His mouth created an incredible pull that made her gasp and lifted her hips toward him.

Every feeling, every impulse, every fiber inside her was straining to get closer to something. This was what she wanted, but not enough. And then Drew's hand slid over her stomach, caressing the triangle of hair at the apex of her thighs. As he explored her tender flesh with his fingers, he placed kisses along her midriff, descending lower.

Drew could feel the tension in Taylor as it coiled tighter. His fingers opened her, sliding in and out of the moist heat as his thumb plucked at the sensitive nub. As she rode closer to the edge he felt his own need growing. He wanted to be inside her when she climaxed. He wanted her to hold on to him as she rode out the storm. Gently he kissed the dark curls and slowed the rhythm of his manipulation. He had to stop now before he forgot.

Her sound of disappointment almost did him in. Reaching across her, Drew snatched open a drawer and pulled out a foil packet, then he sheathed himself. Any doubts he had about her being ready dissolved when he knelt between her legs. She was still damp, her hips tilted to take him.

Drew closed his eyes and steadied himself as he pushed into her, the first touch bringing a rush of sensation as warm velvet closed around his tip. The first stroke was slow as he filled her, allowing himself to explore the inner contours of her body. When he finally sank home, they both exhaled the breath they'd been holding.

Taylor's eyes were closed, but the expression on her face blew away Drew's control. He withdrew and stroked again, harder this time, quicker, deeper. She caught and encouraged the rhythm, which took them where they wanted to go much too quickly, but neither of them seemed to care. This first time had nothing to do with logic and everything to do with need. They both needed release.

Drew called her name hoarsely when it came, and Taylor felt as if a million points of light were shooting along her nerve endings, illuminating her soul. Together they reached for and caught the stars.

ELEVEN

Each time she reached for him in the night, Drew welcomed her, loved her, and didn't ask for promises or explanations of why she'd changed her mind about deepening their relationship. He had already guessed why Taylor needed to touch him, be touched by him. She wanted reassurance—certainty. She wanted that moment when he was inside her, when her body could convince her heart that they belonged together. And he wanted that moment just as much as she did.

The house was quiet around them, and Taylor was pressed against him in her sleep, content and trusting. Drew wanted the moment to last, but daylight was beginning to steal the darkness. When the world began to stir, so would Taylor's doubts. He couldn't put off waking her, he decided unhappily. Noah would be stirring soon, too, and he needed some time to talk to Taylor first. He needed to slip in under her guard, before she had time to push him away again.

Carefully Drew shifted until he could lean on his elbow and look down at her. She protested the change of position with a furrowed brow and sleepy frown, but when she opened her eyes, the frown softened. A shy smile replaced it.

"I wondered what waking up with you would be like," he told her as his finger traced the rosy crescent of a nipple that peeked out from beneath the covers.

Modestly, she pulled the plaid flannel sheet up to her neck and blushed deeply enough that he could tell even in the faint light. Her hands swiped at her eyes, trying to rub off the traces of mascara that were left. "Careful what you wish for. This face in the morning ought to be enough to scare anybody."

"Or addict them," he said softly as he hooked a leg over hers and pulled her into him, adjusting so she was partially beneath him.

Taylor's heart thudded out of control. She wasn't ready for him to be serious, hadn't thought past satisfying the physical need that had gripped her last night. She hadn't known she could want someone so badly that she ached. Making love to Drew had filled up parts of her she hadn't even known were empty and cold.

She felt as if she'd been waiting for the moment all her life, but instead of feeling elated, she felt an almost unbearable disappointment. It was like waking up Christmas morning to the present you desperately wanted and then finding out it was broken or the wrong size. Right now he was looking at her with that I'm-about-to-say-something-important expression. She put her fingers against his mouth and shook her head.

Drew might say the words, but they wouldn't be for her. They were for the woman who made his child happy. They were for Doc Holiday.

Drew was caught up in a seasonal euphoria, and some of that joy had spilled over onto his feelings for her. When the fairy dust of Christmas settled, he'd be back to normal. He'd be back to wanting little Taylor Bishop in his life not because he loved her desperately but because his son needed a mother and she was qualified for the job. Taylor began to regret her foolishness. If she'd been smart, she never would have forgotten her rules about men with children.

Pulling away, Drew ignored her plea for silence. "I was about to say something important."

"No you weren't. Don't say anything. You're confused." She scooted away from him, dragging most of the sheet with her, and settled back against the headboard. "Christmas does that to people. It makes them feel all warm and fuzzy, but it doesn't last. You're in love with that picture-book Christmas family you have in your mind."

"Christmas doesn't have a damn thing to do with it, Taylor." He sat up, the sheet barely covering him. "I want you, not a picture book. I thought I proved that last night."

"You want me to say the sex was good?" She shrugged her shoulders and conceded the point. "The sex was good."

"The sex was great," he corrected, "but that's not what I meant and you know it. I'm trying to tell you that I love you."

"No you don't," she said immediately. She knew better than to let that idea catch hold of her emotions. That would be fatal. "Not really. Trust me."

"Let me get this straight." Drew held up an index finger and swiped his tongue across his bottom lip. "You think I'm going to come to my senses as soon as Christmas is done and realize I'm not really in love with you, that I was only in love with an ideal in my head."

"That pretty much sums it up." She pushed her hair back, trying to rearrange it in some semblance of order, so she'd look calm and rational. "Falling into bed with me kind of completes the image you had when you came to find me."

Instead of the argument she expected, he only nodded his head and slid his legs over the side of the bed. He grabbed his trousers and pulled them on. Then he pulled a T-shirt out of a drawer. Every movement he made was deliberate, controlled. When he finally turned around, she recognized the determination that was etched into his expression. This was the man who planned and waited and got what he wanted. The slow smile he gave her made her heart turn over.

"That was a hundred years ago. When I came to find you, I didn't have a clue about how to love someone or what made a family. Now I do. Six kids and a fireplace full of stockings don't make a family. You taught me that. Last night I figured out that all I want for Christmas is you and Noah. All I want *after* Christmas is you and Noah." Drew unlocked and opened the bedroom door. "I'm not confused, Taylor darlin', but you can think that if it makes you feel safe. You keep telling yourself that I don't mean it every time I make love to you. You keep telling yourself that I'm going to get tired of touching you. You keep telling yourself that the light in here"—he tapped his chest—"is going to go out when I unplug the Christmas tree."

After he left, Taylor stared at the door for a long time. She didn't feel safe at all. She felt ambushed by the sincerity in his voice. Suddenly she was damned if she did and damned if she didn't. Believing Drew meant giving up her life. Believing him meant school plays and PTA meetings. It meant pacing the floor waiting for fevers to break or for Noah to come home after a date. It meant jumping when the phone rang late at night and doing a mental head count to see who was home and who wasn't and expecting the worst when you picked up the phone.

Believing Drew would put her right back where she started thirteen years ago.

The price for believing Drew was just too high. She couldn't.

Slowly she dressed and went downstairs. She stopped in the entrance hall and struggled with herself. Common sense told her to go home, but she couldn't do that either. She couldn't believe, and she couldn't walk away. Not until after Christmas. She'd promised Noah.

Heading for the kitchen, she could see Noah from the back as he sat down at his customary place at the breakfast table, his cereal ready and waiting. She heard the scrape of the skillet on the stove and Drew's question. "Are you sure you don't want some French toast?"

"Yep. Tell me about the kids again."

"What kids?"

"Taylor's kids." Noah carefully perched Bear in the middle of the table. "The ones that need stuff. Why don't they have stuff? We have lots of stuff."

She felt a momentary twinge of sympathy for Drew. He'd just had one complex conversation this morning. She wasn't sure he was up to another one, but he did his best to explain about medical bills and lost jobs and not having enough money to eat, about having to choose between a warm coat and a new toy.

"So Taylor's toy factory is like the check we sent," Noah said. "Except it's stuff, not dollars."

"Right." Drew smiled. "It's stuff, not dollars."

"Stuff?" Taylor asked with a laugh as she finally stepped into the kitchen, pretending she hadn't overheard.

"The float donations," Drew answered, relief flooding through him.

After his little parting speech she'd looked distinctly like a woman who'd had the wind knocked out of her. He hadn't been sure whether he'd pushed too hard or not hard enough. He'd half expected her to sneak out the front door, but here she was standing in his kitchen.

"Why are you here?" Noah asked, homing in on the important issue and breaking the silence.

"She spent the night," Drew said simply. His eyes never left Taylor. "She was too tired to go home."

"Oh." Noah lost interest and began to peel his banana.

"You could take a lesson from him," Drew told her softly as he turned the toast.

"How's that?" she asked, wandering closer.

But not too close, Drew noted. "He believes me when I tell him something."

"He believes in Santa Claus," she whispered as he handed her a plate. "I don't."

Drew held on to the plate an extra few seconds as he whispered, "Not believe in Santa Claus? You might as well not believe in fairies. Or love."

A pregnant silence built in the room until he let go of the plate, breaking the tension. Or at least letting it ebb for the moment.

By five o'clock every business in town was closed. The band and the homemade floats were staged in the high school parking lot, ready to start down Main Street. The toy factory was in front, always the lead float so people could get rid of their donations and have their hands free to clap for their friends and relatives. Anyone who wanted to march in the parade could. All that was required was a five-dollar fee to city hall and a costume, a musical instrument, or a float.

"Taylor, you've checked everything and everyone twice. It's time to go," Drew prodded gently. "It's a volunteer parade. It doesn't have to be perfect."

Guiltily she looked up at him. When he'd shown up, she'd felt a surge of relief and put him right to work, knowing that whatever she missed, he would fix. He'd been answering questions, pushing floats, helping people into candy cane costumes, and generally making her job immeasurably easier for the last hour.

"I guess you're right," she said with a sigh.

"Of course I'm right. The Three Musketeers are saving us a place near the end of the route so we can get there in time to see the whole parade."

"Yeah. Roxie, Noah, and Bear."

He looked up as the toy factory began to move out. "Assuming we go *now*, we won't miss anything."

"Geez, you get awfully pushy."

"Lady, this is not pushy. I have been on my best behavior today," he promised.

And he had. Sometime during the day they'd found a balance in their fragile relationship. Without ever actually discussing the subject, he had agreed not to pressure her and she had agreed not to push him away.

He grabbed her arm and steered her toward the football field, which provided an excellent shortcut to the other side of the parade circuit. They arrived in plenty of time. Noah's face lit up at the sight of them, and he waved. "They're here, Roxie."

"Well, it's about time. I can see a float turning the corner down there," Roxie scolded them as they walked up. "This young man's about to bust his buttons, he's so excited and proud."

Taken aback, Taylor echoed, "Proud?"

"He worked on the float," Roxie explained. "He's been telling me all about it."

Taylor grinned. "Oh."

"So you're excited, huh?" asked Drew as he swept his son up in his arms for a better view.

Noah nodded and reached down to tap Taylor on the shoulder. Then he pointed. Two blocks away, being slowly pulled by David's truck, was the toy factory. Football players dressed like elves were taking the donations and some good-natured ribbing from the spectators. As the float grew closer, Noah began to get restless.

Setting him down, Drew was puzzled by his son's behavior. Noah looked expectantly at Taylor and then at him, waiting for something, looking at their hands and then at Roxie's. Anxiously, he asked, "Where's our stuff?"

Drew knelt down to hear better. "What?"

"Where's our stuff? To put on the float?"

Casting a glance up at Taylor, Drew was hoping for a miracle, but there wasn't one. She shook her head. They'd both been so busy working to get the parade staged that they hadn't had time or the free hands to fool with anything else. "We didn't bring anything, buddy."

"Oh." Unhappily Noah looked at the float again, which was now only about twenty feet away.

Drew stood up and rubbed his hands over his eyes, wishing they'd thought to bring something small. He started to say as much to Taylor when she put a hand on his arm. She was staring at Noah with a look of wonder on her face.

He'd taken a couple of steps into the street, and Drew's first reaction was to pull him back, but Taylor stopped him. "Let him go."

"What do you—" And then understanding dawned.

His son was about to give Bear to someone who needed him more.

Noah hugged Bear tight, then kissed him on the nose to say good-bye. Gravely he held Bear up as the float rumbled past, but he wasn't quite tall enough. Swiftly Drew joined his son, lifting Noah up so he could give them Bear. Drew wasn't sure he could ever be prouder of his son than he was at this moment. Noah knew how to give more than he took. He knew how to care.

"You've still got me," Drew whispered. Noah nodded his head.

When they turned around, Noah's chin was crumpled, but he didn't cry. Taylor did that as she said, "That's the bravest thing I ever saw."

As they stepped back to the curb Noah held out his arm to her as he had the night they decorated the tree. This time when she joined him in the circle of Drew's embrace there was no peace and contentment—only doubt. Doubts about the empty carefree life she had fought so hard to create.

Normally, Taylor loved the quiet Christmas Eve service, especially when it snowed. It was a time of private reflection, an oasis of comfort amid the chaos of a Bishop Christmas. But tonight nothing seemed to calm the jumble of strong emotions inside her.

Blood rushed to her cheeks as she thought of last night. She and Drew had had sex in a house full of people. In her father's house at that. How was it possible for one man to invent so many creative ways to be alone?

Irreverently she grinned as she thought once again of the small lump of coal she intended to slip in Drew's stocking when she went over to exchange presents tonight. He'd been very, very bad last night after the parade. They'd all come back to the Bishop house to demolish the leftovers from the caroling party. The only thing Drew had demolished was her self-control.

If that didn't qualify as very, very bad, she didn't know what did. Drew acted more like a man looking for a lover than a man looking for a mother. She hugged the thought to herself as tightly as Noah had hugged Bear the last time. She didn't want Christmas to end this year, and maybe it wouldn't have to.

Instinct made her look up and toward the wide middle aisle of the church. Drew and Noah, all scrubbed up and handsome in their suits, were scanning the crowd. They smiled when they found her.

As soon as they approached the pew, the family rearranged itself to make enough room by Taylor for them. Drew felt a familiar gratitude, the same kind he'd felt years ago when they'd made room for him in their family. Their acceptance was unquestioning and complete.

By the end of the service, Noah was in Taylor's lap, and Drew knew that he was going to break their unspoken agreement and ask her to marry him. He'd keep asking her until she said yes. Surely once the rush of Christmas morning was over, she'd believe his marriage proposal didn't come from the Christmas spirit.

Struck by a thought, Drew looked around him, at the stained glass, at the vaulted ceiling, at wood polished until it shone. Smiling, he thought perhaps the spirit of Christmas had something to do with his finding Taylor after all. Silently he thanked his guardian angel for pointing him in the right direction.

Later he thanked his guardian angel again as he waited for Taylor to arrive for the gift exchange. Noah's excitement was contagious. He sat on the living room floor, looking longingly at the packages beneath the double-pointed tree as if he couldn't believe he was finally going to get to open one.

"Just the presents Taylor brought over earlier," Drew cautioned from his spot on the couch. "And not until she gets here."

"Yes, sir. I'm just gonna look."

Drew almost laughed. To Noah, a "look" meant weighing, measuring, shaking, holding it up to the light, and peeking in the edges. "You look carefully. Oops! No time for that. Taylor's here."

Racing to the door, Noah wrestled with it to get it open and dragged Taylor in by the hand as she said, "Ho, ho, ho."

"Hurry. The presents are waiting."

Laughing, she said, "Can they wait long enough for me to get my coat off and warm up?"

"Oh. I guess so."

"Warming her up will only take a minute, buddy," Drew promised, and closed the door. He took her coat by the collar and pulled it off, intentionally letting his knuckles skim over her bare back. "You didn't have to dress up, but I'm glad you did."

He whispered in her ear, "Tell me you got the Christmas spirit and you're wearing stockings and a garter belt underneath that drop-dead dress."

She blushed. She was.

"There, all warmed up," pronounced Drew. He tossed her coat over the banister. "Time for presents."

Taylor fought a smile and gave up. She let the men lead her into the living room and settle her in a chair. "Noah first."

"Okay," Drew said, and pulled out a shirt-box-sized packaged wrapped in shiny blue paper and decorated with an intersection of tiny cars.

Immediately Noah carefully pulled off the cars and put them safely on the coffee table so they wouldn't get lost. "Thank you, Taylor."

"You're welcome. Now rip it open. That's half the fun."

He looked up uncertainly, so she nodded her head, giving him permission. Drew hunkered down beside him and watched with interest. When Noah finally got the box open, his eyes popped open, too, and his mouth made a perfect circle.

"Oh, Daddy, look! It's Batman," he said. As he grabbed the contents and stood up, he let the box fall out of his lap. Unfolding the superhero pajamas, he measured them against himself. "Can I wear them to-night?"

"Of course you can! That's what they're for."

"My mother always gave us a new pair of pajamas

every Christmas." She looked at Drew and added with a grin, "That's so we would look good in the pictures Daddy took the next morning instead of like ragamuffins. Your turn."

When he opened the silk robe and burst out laughing, Taylor laughed right along with him. The garment was decorated with the zany cartoon characters of his childhood.

"Good one, Mouse."

"I thought so."

"Now you." Still shaking his head, Drew dropped his robe back in the box and extracted two boxes from beneath the tree. "The top one is from Noah."

"I made it," he volunteered in a small voice.

"You did?" Taylor opened the box expecting to praise anything she found, whether it was wonderful or not. Speechless, Taylor laid aside the top lid and lifted the wreath out.

"Roxie helped, but I glued."

A number of green felt cutouts of Noah's hand were overlapped and glued to a circle of stiff poster board, so that the hands looked like Christmas greenery. A red bow crowned the top and on the trailing ends was written *Noah* and *1994*. When Taylor looked up and smiled, she held out her arms.

Squeezing him tight, she said, "It's wonderful. No one ever made me a wreath. I'm going to keep it for always."

"Whew!" Noah said. "I was afraid one of those brothers would have made you one."

Startled, Taylor paused in the middle of putting the wreath away. "No . . . no, they didn't."

Drew took the wreath and box out of her hand. "We need to hurry this along, 'cause Noah's got to get to bed before Santa flies over. Open this one."

"Why are you so anxious? Does it explode?"

Noah giggled. "Daddy wouldn't give you a bomb."

"I don't know about that," she teased, making a show of unwrapping the box carefully and cracking the lid enough to pull back the tissue paper. Her gasp was audible as she slammed the lid back down and said, "I got pajamas too."

"What color?" Noah asked.

Clear was the first thought that came to mind. Trouble was the second thought. And she knew all about trouble. It was standing a few feet away, looking all satisfied and sexy.

Her next thought was that she could get used to trouble.

Ignoring Noah's question, she glanced at her watch. "Oh, my! Look at the time. Quick, you've got to get to bed before Santa gets here." With that she hustled him up to bed just as she and Drew had planned.

She didn't realize how much tension she had built up inside her until she hesitated to go back downstairs. Hovering on the landing, she discovered she was a coward. If she went down, she'd be one step closer to finishing the job she set out to do. And she didn't want to be finished. It wasn't a job anymore. She wanted to drag everything out as long as possible. She wanted to put off that inevitable moment when Drew realized he didn't really love her after all.

"Psst!" Drew hissed from his study, only his head extending into the hall. "Is he asleep? Hello?"

She started down the stairs, and halfway down she angled her body so he could see her. "Psst, yourself. Are you ready? He's sound asleep up there."

Taking a deep breath, Drew waited for her to get down and then stepped out into the hall. He tiptoed carefully in the heavy black boots so he wouldn't wake his son. When he stopped beside Taylor's silently shaking, doubled-over body, he said, "I don't appreciate your levity."

Getting a grip on herself, she straightened. Drew in a Santa Claus suit was hysterical, but he was also a helluva dad. This was all his idea, and Noah was going to love it. "I wasn't laughing at you."

"I don't see anybody else here."

"I was laughing with you."

"I'm not laughing."

Taylor bit her lip and straightened his belt. She pulled him toward the door. "Come on. Let's get this show on the road."

Trying on his best Santa voice, Drew said, "Ho, ho, ho! How about a kiss for an old man?"

"Whatever will Mrs. Claus say?" Taylor gasped out as he swept her backward.

"She knows I kiss all the pretty girls." He whispered against her lips, "But she's the only one who has my heart."

Drew kissed her then, a quick brush of the lips before he pulled her up and trudged out.

Slowly Taylor pushed the door closed and leaned her forehead against it. Santa wasn't supposed to have wicked eyes like that. Or kiss like that. It was a small kiss, but it melted her heart and made her realize that Drew had done the impossible. He'd made her believe.

She smiled and started for Noah's room. She'd given Drew enough time to get across the street and in position. Now it was her turn to make someone believe.

Pausing in the hallway, after making as much noise as she could without being too obvious, she pretended to talk to Drew. "What? You heard sleigh bells? Don't be silly—"

"Taylor?" Noah called softly.

She went into his room, acting surprised to see him up. "Did you hear it too?"

He sat up and nodded solemnly.

"You did? What was it?"

"Santa."

She tilted her head as though she were listening. "There it is again!" Then she went toward the window, urgently motioning him to follow. "Noah," she whispered his name on one wondrous breath. "It really is Santa."

He joined her eagerly at the window, pressing his face almost up to the glass. Santa was across the street tramping through a yard with a huge bag slung over his shoulder. All of a sudden he looked up at their window and waved. Taylor waved back. Then Santa seemed to look at Noah and make the okay sign. Awed, Noah sat very still, as though he were trying to memorize everything about the moment.

When Santa disappeared around the back of the house, she gently guided Noah back to bed and tucked him in as he gave her a play-by-play of everything they'd seen, even though she'd seen it too. Taylor listened enthusiastically and plumped all his pillows and straightened all his covers.

"And he saw me," Noah whispered again when he was through.

"Which means you'd better get back to sleep before he finishes that side of the block." She dropped a kiss on his cheek and turned to go as she heard the faint noise of a door downstairs. "I'll go get your dad. He's not going to believe this. You have to tell him."

"Taylor?"

"Mmm?"

"Where were the reindeer?"

"Reindeer?" she asked in a squeaky voice, even though she knew exactly which reindeer he meant.

"Santa's reindeer."

"On the roof."

"Nope. I looked."

"Oh . . . well . . . they were . . . flying back for more toys while Santa was inside. Yep, that's it. See, they have magic, and every time Santa goes into a house, they zip back to the North Pole and refill the sleigh. Those elves have a tough job keeping all the packages straight." She turned to leave again.

"Taylor?"

"What?" she asked, chuckling as she faced him. She paused with a hand on the door frame.

"Are you sure that Santa can bring good little boys exactly what they want?"

"I'm sure."

"Are you really sure or maybe sure?"

"I'm really sure," she promised. This time she waited for the next question. The one she knew was coming.

"Do you think I'm a good little boy?"

"I know you're a good little boy." She went to him and touched a finger to his nose. "You're the best. Just like your daddy."

"Who's just like his daddy?" Drew asked, startling Taylor, who obviously hadn't heard him slip up behind her. He hadn't meant to eavesdrop, but something in Noah's voice when he asked for Taylor's opinion kept him quiet. He'd heard enough to know that Noah loved and trusted Taylor. He hadn't needed to hear any more.

"I am. Taylor says."

"Well! If *Taylor* says, it must be true. And why are you up?" he asked his son playfully. "Don't you know that Santa won't come if you're awake?"

"You missed all the excitement," Taylor told Drew. "Get your son to tell you about it. Night, Noah."

"Night, Taylor," he called after her as she left.

She meant to walk away and leave them alone, but Noah's first words to his dad reached right out into the hallway and glued her feet to the floor.

"I saw Mommy kissing Santa Claus."

"What?" She heard all the surprise that she felt echoed in Drew's voice.

"I woke up, and I saw Mommy kissing Santa Claus."

"Here? Tonight?" Drew asked.

She knew they were both thinking about the kiss downstairs.

"Yes, sir. He said Mrs. Claus lets him kiss all the pretty girls."

Taylor clapped a hand over her mouth.

"Mommy's not here," Drew explained patiently. "But Taylor's got blond hair like Mommy. Maybe you saw Taylor kissing Santa Claus. I hear they're old friends. He likes her cookies."

Good stretch, Taylor thought. Definitely deserving of extra credit. Now if Noah would only buy it.

Undaunted, Noah said, "Yep, it *was* Taylor. She's going to be my mommy now. I fixed it all, Daddy. I asked Santa when we went to see him. He gives the good little boys exactly what they want. He and Taylor both said so. So she's going to be my mommy."

Taylor still had a hand over her mouth, but it wasn't to hold back laughter anymore. It was to hold back fear. She didn't even breathe as she waited for Drew's response.

"Well, I want Taylor to be your mommy, too. We need her around here . . ."

Already walking away, she didn't hear the rest. Didn't want to. Didn't need to. Drew really did want her for all the wrong reasons. How could she have let herself believe?

The hurt was so deep, she didn't cry. She couldn't

even take joy from Noah's affection for her. To do that would be to admit that she wanted his affection. Admitting she cared so deeply for a little boy whose real mother abandoned him would only let guilt tear her apart. For once in her life she wanted to choose her future, not be forced into it by guilt.

Seven days ago she'd been absolutely clear about what she wanted—a carefree life of her own—and then she had let Drew confuse her. Grateful she'd come to her senses in time, she focused on the last job she had to do. Then she was going to get as far away from Drew as she could.

She took the cookies off the plate by the fireplace and replaced them with crumbs. She poured the milk down the drain and put the glass back beside the plate. Drew would have to handle putting out Santa Claus's gifts. Picking up her purse from the coffee table, she looked around. Symbols of a joyous season were everywhere. She was the one who'd put them there.

"Bah, humbug," she whispered, and then cursed as she heard Drew's footsteps pounding down the stairs. She hadn't been quick enough.

Drew was grinning when he came in, rubbing his hands and looking a lot like he was going to kiss her. "I love Christmas."

"That makes one of us."

His grin faltered and so did he. "Come again?"

Coward that she was, Taylor opted for the easy way out. All she wanted was to get out the door and into her car. He couldn't follow her then. Not with Noah in the house. "Don't mind me. I'm tired. I thought I might go home early for a change."

"Wait." Drew's hand circled her arm as she went by, and he pulled her to him. "I was going to ask you this tomorrow, but Noah has convinced me I need to settle this on Christmas Eve."

Inside, Taylor went cold and numb. It was the only way she could survive the next few minutes. He was really going to do it. He was going to ask her to marry him. *Because his son wanted a mother.*

His hands cupped her face as he said, "Marry me, Taylor. It's unanimous. We're head over heels in love with you."

"Unanimous?" She jerked her head out of his hands, his choice of words finally pushing the hurt inside her toward anger. "Since when can you take a vote on love? Noah's approval isn't enough for me. It never was."

"Whoa, wait a minute—" The shock on his face looked good enough to be real.

"Save it, Drew. I heard. Noah wants a mother for Christmas, and you're going to get him one."

"You heard," Drew repeated, beginning to catch on. "If you're going to eavesdrop at least hang around for the good parts, darlin'."

Taylor slung the strap of her purse over her shoulder. "I heard all the good parts I could stand for one conversation."

"I don't think so. If you'd stuck around you would have heard me tell Noah that we didn't need you half as much as you needed us." He reached out, but she pulled away. That hurt him almost as much as the way she jumped to conclusions.

"Dammit, Taylor, I told Noah that we had to give you more love than we took because that's how it was when you really loved someone. I learned that from you. That's why I love you."

"No." Taylor didn't want to listen. Tears were too close to the surface. The anger brought them out. "I don't want to argue about this. I want to go home. Don't make this difficult. You owe me. I've done what you asked."

"And more."

Taylor's head snapped up. "Touché."

A groan of frustration escaped him. "Taylor, stop twisting everything I say because you *think* you hear something that isn't there to hear!"

"What I heard upstairs was a man who loves his son and wants to make him happy. No matter what the cost." A tear slipped out. She ignored it.

"And I can't love you because I love Noah?" he asked, incredulous.

"Bingo."

"That's not fair."

"Fair?" She flicked the tear away as it trailed down her cheek. "Who the hell said life was fair? It sure wasn't fair when my mother died. It sure wasn't fair when I had to help raise my brothers. And it sure as hell isn't fair now. You love the idea of the *three* of us. What happens when he grows up and doesn't need me anymore?"

"*I'll* still need you! I'll still love you. I'm not one of

your brothers!" He almost shouted the denial. "I'm not asking you to repeat the past, Taylor. I'm asking you to create a future. And that future includes Noah. Listen to what I'm saying. *I love you.* Hell, I think I've loved you half my life. The only question is—do you love me?"

In a split second he'd turned the argument upside down. Suddenly he wasn't the one on the defensive. She was, and she didn't like it. "No, I don't."

"Liar." The accusation was rapid-fire and firm, without a hint of apology.

He was right. She was lying, but that lie and her pride were the only things that could get her out the door in one piece. She didn't bother to argue; she couldn't because she'd never been able to fool Drew. Instead she walked away, picked up her coat from the banister, and left.

Helplessly Drew watched her go, knowing nothing he could say would make a difference right now. Even if it would, he couldn't follow her. He couldn't leave Noah alone in the house. And she knew it.

The urge to cry was an amazing thing, Taylor realized. It was a conditioned response. You got hurt, you cried. Crying was supposed to make it better, but this time crying would only make it hurt worse. And then, when she was finished crying, there wouldn't be anyone to tuck her in. No one to promise her everything would be all right. There hadn't been anyone for a long time.

Pulling herself together, she held her index fingers

beneath her eyes until the urge passed. Then she unlocked the front door and slipped inside. The house was dark. It was close to midnight.

And all through the house not a creature was stirring, except for this mouse, she thought bleakly. She shed her coat and rubbed her arms against the chill in the house.

"You're out late," a masculine voice observed.

Taylor jumped and clutched the front of her dress. "Dad! You scared me." Her eyes adjusted to the dark, and she could see him sitting in a chair, staring at the tree. She joined him. "What are you doing skulking around in the dark?"

"Playing Santa Claus."

"The stockings," she said, and sat down on the couch. Her dad always filled the stockings, refused to quit even when his kids got married. He just bought the spouse a stocking.

"Yeah," he confirmed. "I had a scare there for a minute. I couldn't find yours."

"Oh, right. It's in my box." She started to get it.

"No. I found it."

"You did?"

He laughed. "Well, don't sound so shocked! Your old dad is more resourceful than you've ever given me credit for. But I guess that's as much my fault as it is yours." He yawned and heaved himself out of the chair. "I'm beat. You going to bed now?"

"In a minute. I want to stay down here and look at the tree for a while."

"G'night, baby. Merry Christmas."

"Merry Christmas." Suddenly she reached out and

caught his hand, stopping him. "Dad, what's as much your fault as it is mine?"

He looked surprised. "I was talking about how you think it's your job to take care of us. I let you shoulder too much responsibility when your mother died. That part was my fault. Can't change it now, but I wish I could."

"And what part is my fault?" she asked reluctantly.

He patted her cheek. "Baby, you inherited your mother's gift for loving people right along with her need to take care of 'em. You've always had some picture in your head of how everything should be, and God help anyone who messed up the picture or refused to be happy."

"I wasn't that bad," she argued, willing him to agree. When he didn't say anything, she asked, "Was I?"

An awkward silence stretched long enough to give her an answer, but her dad softened the truth by saying, "I don't want you to change, if that's what you're worried about. How could I? It's the reason I fell in love with your mother."

"Because she loved her family?"

"No." He winked. "Because I knew she could love me. Night, Taylor."

"Good night," she whispered again. The chill she felt now had nothing to do with the temperature. It was the kind of chill a person got when they realized they'd made a horrible mistake in judgment.

All around her was evidence that the family had done just fine without her help this Christmas. All the presents had been bought; all the cookies baked; and the tree trimmed. All those years, if she hadn't created the holiday memories, someone else would have. If she hadn't ironed the boys' shirts, they would have worn them right out of the dryer and been happy about it.

Her dad was right. All those sacrifices she thought she'd been making for them weren't really sacrifices. She wanted those memories. She wanted the boys to know they were loved. Everything she'd accused Drew of—falling in love with the idea of being a family, wanting a picture-book Christmas, wanting Noah to be loved—all those things were also true of her. In spades.

At the very least she owed him an apology for being the pot who called the kettle black. She'd let her pride get all mixed up with her emotions. So much so that she forgot the lesson Martha taught her. A man's wife meant a lot more to him than a sister. Drew wanted a wife. He wanted to find some love and hold on to it forever.

Taylor put her head in her hands and closed her eyes against the painful realizations that battered her heart. Drew had stood in this very room and confessed his parents hadn't loved him. No one had ever loved him, not the way he wanted to be loved. Not the way Drew believed she could love him. He'd fallen in love with her for the same reason her dad had fallen in love with her mother.

Pulling in a ragged breath, Taylor looked up at the angel on the tree. She was closer than the stars. "How am I going to make this right?"

And then she knew.

Drew splashed water on his face, but didn't bother to put his new robe on over his pajama bottoms. It reminded him of Taylor, and right now he didn't need any more reminders of what he couldn't have. He'd been reminded too many times last night, every time he'd reached for her and she wasn't there. About four o'clock in the morning he gave up on sleep, gave up on reaching.

Now that the sun was almost up, he needed coffee. With any luck caffeine would stimulate his imagination, and then he'd know what to say to Noah about why they weren't going to the Bishops' for Christmas dinner. Silently he passed his son's room and resisted the urge to wake him. The sooner Noah woke up, the sooner the questions about Taylor would start. Drew wasn't up to those right now. He wasn't up to much of anything, he decided as he passed the Christmas tree.

Especially since he was hallucinating.

He stopped and closed his eyes, rubbing with his thumb and forefinger. "Taylor, darlin', you've got to get out of my head."

"Why?"

The softly spoken question sent a chill through Drew. Slowly he turned on his heel. He wasn't hallucinating. There she was. She looked like hell and was still the best thing he'd ever seen. His heart began a celebration dance, but his mind was more cautious. He took in the change of clothes, the red and slightly puffy eyes, and the determination in her gaze.

Questions crowded his mind, but the only one that came out was, "How?"

"Spare key." She fished in her jeans pocket. "You gave it to me when you went to get Noah's bike." She held it out. When he wouldn't take it, Taylor put it back in her pocket.

"Why are you here?" His voice was husky.

"I forgot to put something on the tree."

Confused, he looked at the spruce and then back at her. "The tree is fine. You didn't come all the way over here to put an ornament on the tree."

"No, I didn't." She moved so he could see the box at her feet. "I put on twenty-eight of them. I have one left."

Drew closed his eyes and tried to make his mind work. Lack of sleep made it impossible. "I don't understand. That's your box of ornaments. It's supposed to be on your tree."

"This *is* my tree. I love this tree." She pushed up her sleeves and lifted her chin. "I love Noah. I love you. I couldn't imagine being anywhere else on Christmas morning. And if it's not too late, I want to say yes."

An invisible band around Drew's chest loosened. Somewhere between last night and this morning Taylor had found the certainty she was looking for. "Say it again."

She walked toward him and straight into his arms. "I couldn't imagine being anywhere else on Christmas morning."

"No. The other part," he said. "The part about loving me."

"This could take a while," she warned, and arched an eyebrow.

"Do I look like I'm going anywhere?"

"I'm not talking about the next ten minutes. I'm talking about the rest of your life."

"I've got time. Again," he ordered as he kissed the corners of her mouth.

"I love you." Taylor had never meant anything more in her entire life. "The only question is, are you still going to love me when Noah opens that fireman's hat?"

Drew chuckled as he worked his way down her throat. "The loud one with the real siren?"

"Mmm," was all Taylor could manage.

"I can't imagine not loving you." And then he kissed her and didn't stop until Noah came thundering down the stairs. Drew turned Taylor around in his arms so they could both see the expression on Noah's face when he came in.

"A bike! Oh, Daddy!" He was so excited he could barely talk. "I got a bike. How did Santa know? I never even asked for one! All I asked for was Taylor."

"He brought that too, son."

Noah looked up, registered his dad's arms around Taylor, and gave them a lopsided grin. "This is the best Santa Claus ever."

When all the excitement died down, Noah put his "mommy's" crystal star on the tree's second point, and Drew knew he finally had everything he ever wanted—a Taylor Bishop Christmas.

**HIDDEN TREASURES AWAIT YOU IN
LOVESWEPT'S TREASURED TALES III**

WHAT HAPPENS WHEN
LITTLE RED RIDING HOOD
MEETS JACK AND THE BEANSTALK
IN THE GARDEN OF EDEN
WHILE PERFORMING
"TAMING OF THE SHREW"?

STAY TUNED FOR DETAILS
ABOUT OUR UPCOMING CONTEST—
FUN AND PRIZES!

THE EDITOR'S CORNER

We are proud to present TREASURED TALES III—four wonderful romances inspired by classic, well-loved stories written by some of the most talented and popular authors writing women's romantic fiction today. Touching, tender, packed with emotion and wonderfully happy endings, next month's LOVESWEPTs are real treasures.

From the supertalented Glenna McReynolds comes **DRAGON'S EDEN**, LOVESWEPT #726, another tale full of passion and intensity. When Jackson Daniels awakens and meets the gaze of a sensual, silver-eyed angel, he can't decide whether the tropical island is his prison—or sanctuary! Fascinated by the powerful warrior who would have tempted a saint, Sugar feels that she was born to be Eve to his Adam. Once Jackson binds her to him with pleasure in a private paradise, Sugar must keep her beloved renegade safe within the haven of her heart. Glenna proves that the most dangerous adventure of all may be falling in love!

The ever-popular Peggy Webb delivers another terrific romance with **CAN'T STOP LOVING YOU**, LOVESWEPT #727. When Helen Sullivan makes her entrance in a red dress that fits like sin, Brick wants to toss his ex-wife over his shoulder and make love to her until she confesses why she'd left him. He's come seeking revenge, but she is still a fire in his blood—and she can't deny her rough-and-tumble bad boy still possesses her heart. Peggy enchants with this delicious story of madness and mayhem, spiced with laughter and steamy with irresistible passion—Shakespeare's *Taming of the Shrew* was never this sizzling.

Patt Bucheister invites you to indulge in some **HOT SOUTHERN NIGHTS**, LOVESWEPT #728. He is brash, brilliant, and too damn sure of himself, but Brett Southern knows the worst: Sam Horn is no gentleman! Determined to use her historic plantation for his documentary, fascinated by Brett's gorgeous eyes, her hands, her lips, Sam finds he wants to do more than just kiss this beauty in a red cape. Once her handsome wolf draws her into his lair, how long will she make him wait until she surrenders? Writing of playful passion and spellbinding secrets, Patt evokes the sultry, sensual heat that kindles the best kind of love story.

For the truly unique, the delightful Victoria Leigh offers **STALKING THE GIANT**, LOVESWEPT #729. Alex Hastings is more than Mr. Tall, Dark and Interesting, Jacqueline Sommers decides—he is all her secret dreams of England rolled into one gorgeous hunk! Romancing her with flowers, tempting her with wicked kisses that taste of forever, he makes her promise to be his—but Jack will climb the highest height, even a beanstalk, to get her sexy giant to admit what he feels for her is love. If true romance is the ultimate fairy tale, then Victoria celebrates its mystery and magic in this delectable story of pursuit and pleasure!

Happy reading!

With warmest wishes,

Beth de Guzman

Senior Editor

P.S. Don't miss the women's novels coming your way in February: **VALENTINE,** by bestselling author Jane Feather, is the newest historical romance brimming with passion and intrigue in the blockbuster tradition of Amanda Quick; **PRINCE OF DREAMS,** from the highly acclaimed Susan Krinard, is a spellbinding romance in which a beautiful woman risks the ultimate temptation . . . love with the sensual vampire who's invaded her dreams; **FIRST LOVES,** by Jean Stone, is a wonderful women's novel about three thirty-something women who rediscover their first loves—with devastating consequences. We'll be giving you a sneak peek at these terrific books in next month's LOVESWEPTs. And immediately following this page, look for a preview of the exciting romances from Bantam that are *available now!*

Don't miss these exciting books by your
favorite Bantam authors

On sale in December

HEAVEN'S PRICE
by Sandra Brown

LORD OF ENCHANTMENT
by Suzanne Robinson

SURRENDER TO A STRANGER
by Karyn Monk

HEAVEN'S PRICE
by
SANDRA BROWN

AVAILABLE IN HARDCOVER

"Ms. Brown's larger than life heroes and heroines make you believe all the warm, wonderful, wild things in life."
—*Rendezvous*

With one huge bestseller after another, Sandra Brown has earned a place among America's most popular romance writers. Now the New York Times bestselling author of TEMPERATURES RISING brings us this classic, sensuous novel filled with her trademark blend of humor and passion, about a woman who thought she knew her destiny until she learns that fate—and her heart—have something else in store.

LORD OF ENCHANTMENT
by
Suzanne Robinson

With every fiber of her being, Penelope Fairfax knew that she should run . . . but she couldn't abandon the achingly handsome stranger who'd washed up on her jagged shore. No doubt he was like the other men she'd come to Penance Isle to escape—the rash warriors whose reckless swordplay left her trembling with fear. Yet when this virile castaway awoke with no memory of who he was, she couldn't turn him away, no matter the havoc he would wreak on her peace—or to her heart. . . .

"Where have you been?" he snapped. "Jesu, woman, my stomach is shriveled with hunger."

Pen's hesitant demeanor vanished in a flare of answering temper. She marched up the steps and stood in front of him, arms folded across her chest.

"If you're strong enough to bellow like an ox in rut, sirrah, you're strong enough to descend to the hall and eat with the rest of us."

Tristan narrowed his eyes and took in the rise and fall of her breasts. He hadn't felt so stirred in—he had no idea how long. Letting his sheet fall a little lower on his hips, he stepped close to her, so close he could feel her heat, and said in a growl, "By the cross, lady, if you'll have me in this sheet, I'll oblige you."

Pen's gaze flew from his eyes to his chest, and then down to the warm, smooth skin of his hip. She made a little sound, then stumbled backward, her color rising. Her step took her to the brink of the stairs, where she tottered and cried out. Her fragile features contorted with terror. Tristan swore and grabbed for her with both hands. The sheet fell as he grasped her by the arms, swept her against the wall and pressed against her as if to prevent her from plummeting down the black steepness with the force of his weight.

They remained pressed against each other, he panting with relief, she shivering with leftover fear. Then she gave a squawk and shoved at his chest.

"Don't touch me!"

She writhed against him, and he felt himself stir. Heedless of the blows with which she was now buffeting him, he set his jaw and tried not to succumb to this sudden arousal. He heard her curse him. Her body twisted. Her hip ground into his unruly part, causing it to leap and buck. He gasped. If he didn't stop her, he would lose all chivalry and lift her skirts right here on the landing. He felt himself twitch again. Catching hold of her upper arms, he lifted her abruptly and gave her a gentle shake that bumped her head against the wall.

"Be still, damn you."

She gaped at him, quivering. Slowly he lowered her to her feet. Their bodies slid over each other, and he gritted his teeth as the slight curve of her breasts caressed his bare shoulder and chest. Her legs slithered down his own, and his rigid sex danced into her skirt, seeking her warmth. Wordlessly she continued to stare at him in consternation.

He couldn't help it. As she settled on her feet, he pressed against her and lowered his head. Using his own special name for her, he whispered hoarsely, "You should take better care, Gratiana." He moved his hips against her and elicited a quick indrawing of breath from her. "Look what happens when you neglect me."

She squirmed and turned her head aside, but he found her mouth anyway. She tried to keep her mouth closed. He smiled against her lips and snaked his hand up to cup her breast. When her mouth opened for a gasp, his tongue invaded. She stiffened, then caught her breath as he began to suck on her.

Tristan felt her body soften, felt her lips

open to him. He was brushing his hips back and forth against her when she tore her lips from his.

"No, please."

He heard fear. The music of her voice was drowned by it. Whatever he might be, he was certain he wasn't a man of rapine and forced submission.

"Aye, Gratiana. A moment."

Tristan turned his face away, setting his hot cheek on hers, and gulped in deep breaths. Then he lifted his head to look into her alarmed eyes and gave her a pained smile.

"If you wish to avoid such encounters, I advise you to find me clothing, Mistress Fairfax."

"Oh."

"Aye, chuck. Now, if you will close your eyes, I'll return to my chamber. But if I'm not clothed and fed in the space of an hour, I'll come looking for you as I am, with no sheet."

"No!"

Her outrage made him chuckle. He stepped away from her. Pen's glance darted down, as he'd known it would. She turned the color of a rose, gave a small whimper, and squeezed her eyes shut. Taking pity on her, he turned, picked up his sheet, and vanished into his chamber. She must have opened her eyes quickly, for she banged the door shut after him.

He heard the tap of her slippers on the stone stairs as she fled. Glancing down at himself, Tristan sighed. He went to a wash-bowl resting on a sideboard and splashed icy water on his face and chest. He spent the next few minutes calming his rampant urges. By the time Mistress Fairfax knocked on his door, he was resting in bed again with the covers drawn up to his chest.

"Enter, Gratiana, if you dare."

SURRENDER TO A STRANGER
by
Karyn Monk

She trusted him with her life—but could she trust him with her heart?

Sentenced to death, Jacqueline never expected a daring rescue from her filthy cell by an unlikely visitor whose disguise hid a devastatingly handsome British agent. Now the two were on the run —and for as long as he was there to protect her, she felt strangely safe. . . .

Jacqueline seated herself in the chair. It was hard and extremely uncomfortable. She twisted and turned in it a few times to see if she could find a more restful position. She could not. She repositioned herself again, leaned back, folded her arms across her chest and gritted her teeth, determined that, comfortable or not, she was going to sleep. Within a few minutes her whole body began to quiver. Now that she had stopped moving, she realized the room was unbearably cold. She would have to stumble around in the dark again to find her jacket, which was coarse and filthy and smelled offensive.

Loud snoring was rising from the mound on the bed. It was quite evident that Citizen Julien, or whoever he was, had not encountered the least bit of difficulty in falling asleep. Despite the fact that his shoulders were bare, he was evidently quite comfortable. Of course, he did have the advantage of a sheet and blanket.

Noiselessly slipping out of her wooden sabots, she crept through the darkness over to the bed. Citizen Julien did not stir but continued his deep, even snoring. Jacqueline let out a small breath of relief.

The problem was that his hand actually gripped the blanket, making it impossible for her to move it without his knowledge. She would have to get him to loosen his hold before she could proceed. She took a step closer to him and bent down low. With one hand firmly grasping the blanket and her lips positioned just inches away from his ear, she shaped her mouth into a tiny circle and very gently began to blow, a soft, fluttering little breath that made the length of hair lying against his ear begin to dance and tickle him. At first he merely frowned, his eyebrows knitting together in profound irritation. She blew a little harder, and to her delight his hand released the blanket and moved up to scratch the offending ear. Quick as a whip she yanked down the blanket and clutched it to her chest. His tickling problem solved, the stranger sighed and contentedly laid his arm on his chest. Barely able to contain her smugness, Jacqueline turned from the bed to wrap herself in her prize.

Strong hands clamped around her waist with an iron grip, and before she knew what she was about she was sailing through the air and landed with a thud on the mattress beside him. He held her down with one hand and looked at her with amusement.

"There are two lessons you have learned tonight," he remarked. "The first, never assume your opponent is sleeping, unless you have drugged him or knocked him over the head. The second, if it is at all possible, make sure you get a decent night's sleep." Still holding her down, he disentangled her from the blanket and arranged it over both of them. Then he lowered himself to the mattress and casually flung his arm over her, effectively pinning her to the bed. "Now be a good mademoiselle and show me how well you have learned the second lesson," he finished, in much the same tone one would use on a naughty child.

"Let me go!" Jacqueline ordered as she struggled against his hold and tried to sit up.

His response was to tighten his arm around her and haul her even closer against his body.

"It was warmth you were seeking, was it not?" he demanded roughly. "You waste your energy and precious sleep with this nonsense. We still have far to go before you are safe. Lie still and go to sleep." Evidently thinking the matter settled, he closed his eyes.

Mere seconds later a sharp pain assaulted his shoulder, and his eyes flew open to see Jacqueline with her teeth on him.

With a soft oath he pushed her away. "Do you really wish to sleep in the chair that much?" he demanded in a tightly controlled voice.

"It is not that I wish to sleep in the chair, it is that I do not wish to sleep with you!" she hissed.

He was silent for a moment, as if he was somehow confused or surprised by that statement. Suddenly he moved away from her. "Mademoiselle," he began in an incredulous tone, "when exactly was the last time you bathed?"

"How dare you!" Jacqueline spat out as she sat bolt upright on the bed.

"I mean no insult," he swiftly qualified. "It's just that if you are worried about your precious virtue I would like to set your mind at ease. My preference is for women who have bathed at least sometime within the not too distant past. I realize your friend who visited you before me was not quite so discriminating, and perhaps that is what has given you cause for concern." He turned away from her and adjusted his half of the blanket over his shoulder. "You may share this bed with me and rest completely assured that even if you were stark naked and willing, I would not have the slightest desire of laying a hand on you."

A mixture of humiliation and fury boiled up inside Jacqueline. It was true, she realized, she was sorely in need of a bath. But the rooms at La Conciergerie did not include hot water and maid service. How dare this vulgar, low-minded lout comment on the miserable state of her hygiene or tell her boldly that he did not desire her. He was discourteous beyond belief. Still, she had to admit, it did make her feel a little safer. Perhaps in her present condition she truly was offensive enough to repel a man. Well, if so, that suited her perfectly.

"Move over," she ordered sharply as she gave the pillow on what was to be her side a whack.

He sighed impatiently and moved a bit to accommodate her. Jacqueline lay down and primly drew the blanket up to her chin. The space he offered her had already been warmed by the heat of his body. In fact, after a few minutes she found she could feel the heat of him radiating across the scant inches that separated them. It filtered through the coarse wool of her shirt and trousers and warmed her chilled flesh. It had been a long time since she had felt warm in bed.

At home, Henriette used to heat the icy sheets of her enormous bed during the winter with a long-handled brass pan filled with hot coals. That was very nice, but inevitably during the night the effect would wear off and she would find herself huddled beneath a mountain of blankets trying not to move out of the last remaining warm spot. During her long nights at La Conciergerie she had tried unsuccessfully to control the terrible chills that assaulted her every time she crawled into her rickety little trestle bed, fully clothed and with only one thin blanket to offer her any comfort. This unfamiliar sensation of heat was absolutely delicious. It made her very sleepy. She allowed herself a muffled sigh of pleasure and unconsciously huddled closer to its source.

"Good night, mademoiselle."

The unexpected voice jolted her back to wakefulness. With a little gasp she rolled over, moving as far away from him as the limits of the bed would allow.

And don't miss these fabulous romances
from Bantam Books,
on sale in January:

VALENTINE
by the nationally bestselling author

Jane Feather

"An author to treasure."
—*Romantic Times*

PRINCE OF DREAMS
by the highly acclaimed

Susan Krinard

"Susan Krinard has set the standard for
today's fantasy romance."
—*Affaire de Coeur*

FIRST LOVES
by the sensational

Jean Stone

What if you could go back and rediscover
the magic . . .